# CURSE OF THORNS

## WICKED FAE
### BOOK TWO

## STACEY TROMBLEY

# Curse of Thorns

## WICKED FAE

## Book 2

### STACEY TROMBLEY

# 1

## CAELYNN

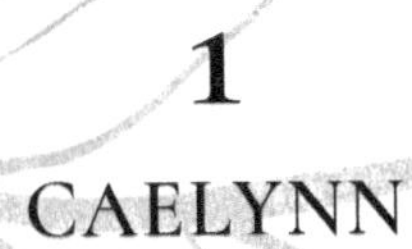

I sit in the darkness, rough bark under my thigh scratching uncomfortably as I peer through the second-floor window into the dorm. Soft yellow light glows within, while inky shadows swallow me outside. Alone.

Always alone.

Magic rushes through my lungs as I breathe. I grip the branch beneath me harder and watch a lovely human girl with raven black hair laughing with her new roommate. She pauses inside the room, her expression falling as her eyes settle on an envelope sitting on her desk.

A gust of wind tosses my hair wildly. It twists around me, caressing my neck. Part of me longs to be inside with her, laughing and dreaming and just being. But if there is one thing I've learned in the last few weeks it's that I don't belong here.

Ever since the trials, I haven't been able to subdue the power roaring through my veins like I could before. Now that I've felt it, embraced it, the magic won't let go of its hold on me. Before the trials I had spent so much time fighting against the darkness inside; the pain made that easy. I'd forgotten who I was. What I am.

Now, it's in everything. Every move I make, everything I see.

This power is taking a life of its own, and the more attention I bring to myself, the more dangerous it is for her.

During Raven's orientation, I'd accidentally glamoured one of the senior boys who made an off-handed comment to her. He spent the rest of the day following us around like a puppy, carrying her books, and opening doors. It was rather annoying—though, Raven loved it. I'd also accidentally wrapped shadows around me and "disappeared" mid-conversation with a girl who asked probing questions about mine and Raven's relationship.

I can't even explain our relationship to her, let alone strangers.

I love her. In so many ways, not just friendship. But also not as a lover. Maybe it's because she's so young, so mortal. Maybe it's because my life is so complicated.

Maybe it's Rev.

I don't know. But regardless of our feelings, there is one thing I know for sure that makes this as simple as breathing. The longer I stay near Raven, the more likely it is she'll get hurt—and I don't mean emotionally.

Rev won't be around to heal her this time.

Tears well in Raven's eyes as she reads my farewell letter. She had to know it was coming, right? I'd stayed with her for the last two months, making sure she's set up and safe. She's been accepted into a great private school on full scholarship—that may have been thanks to a not-so-accidental glamouring—so her last year in the system will be foster-home free. I did not apply to the same school.

We'd talked about me going back to the fae realm soon since my banishment is still temporarily suspended. Maybe she just thought I'd leave and be back periodically. I know she's willing to take the risk in order to see me, but it's easier to risk yourself than to risk someone you love.

Raven is in danger with me around, and I'm not willing to put her at risk. Case and point—the stupid fae-spy that's lurked around campus the last week. Even right now, he's squatting behind a bush by the front door of the dorm rooms. His shaved head practically sparkles in the darkness.

I shake my head, watching him. Luminescent Court fae will never be as good at sleuthing as those from the Shadow Court. I've been watching him, waiting to see if I need to intervene.

Let him try to touch Raven and things will escalate very quickly. As it is, he doesn't even know I've noticed him. So, I'll wait. I've played my part, made it clear I'm leaving. So, when I disappear, will he as well? That's going to mean a few lonely days in the shadows, just watching.

If he leaves, so will I.

If he acts, I will act too.

I lean my head against the base of the tree and close my eyes. He doesn't move for nearly an hour—long enough for Raven to cry herself to sleep. Long enough for me to question every life choice.

When I open my eyes, the spy and his shiny head are gone.

*Dammit.*

My magic stretches out, feeling for any disturbance. Just around the corner, there's a flicker of magic. He didn't get far, then.

I slip into my own shadows, following their pull, slinking through silently, entirely invisible to all but the rare fae trained to see through the magic.

Around the corner, there is still no sign of the spy, no trail at all. Getting a little more resourceful, are we? So if he hasn't moved farther around the building...

My heart pounds harder.

He hasn't ever gone inside the building, he's only lurked. So, if he has now... that would change the game.

———

I clench my hands into hard fists as I tiptoe down the quiet halls. It's near midnight by now, which means all the students are in their dorms pretending to sleep. Classes don't start for another three days. Behind a few doors, whispers and laughter can be heard. Quick breathing behind another—a couple going at it.

My feet make no sound as I cross over the porcelain tiles, dull florescent lights buzz overhead. I feel for magic. I listen for the thud of an eager heart.

*Thump-thump.* I pause.

Raven's door is around the next bend. The feeling and basic bodily sounds are definitely coming from that direction. Is it the spy?

A dark chuckle greets me before I even make the final turn. "I've been watching you." His low voice rumbles through the air.

I stifle a gasp. Well, that answers that question. I pull in a long breath, hold my head high, and turn the corner. Arms crossed, I lean casually against the wall a dozen or so feet from my adversary. "Have you? I hadn't noticed."

Mr. Shiny Head grips a sword in one hand and a dagger in the other. He approaches slowly, eyes pinned to me. His lips curl into a smile, but everything else tells me he's tense. He planned for this confrontation, but he's still anxious.

"You were planning to leave, were you?" he asks. "Abandoning your little friend to fend for herself?"

I narrow my eyes. "I'm the problem. Not her." One part an answer to his question, and one part a threat—leave her the hell out of it.

"That you are. Don't worry, you won't be for much longer." His knees bend ever so slightly, his muscles tense, but before either of us can react, a blade presses against my jugular.

*Dammit.* How had I not noticed the second spy?

For one moment, I'm shocked; the next—I act.

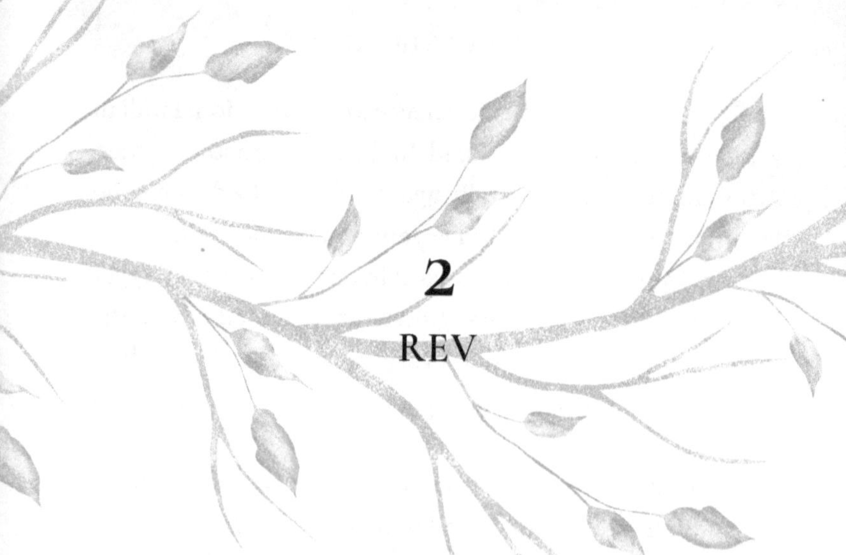

# 2
## REV

The door to the banquet hall swings open and slams against the back wall. The monotone voices of the Luminescent Court royals are hushed in an instant.

Some stop mid-bite to watch the intruder, wide-eyed. The whole court is frozen, even myself, as a blond fae in skinny jeans and thick black boots—our sworn enemy—stomps down the aisle toward the ruling family. Toward me.

Admittedly, the Rev of six months ago would have stood, sword in hand, eager for the chance to remove her beautiful head from her beautiful body. Today... I still don't know what to feel. A desire to kill her is the only thing I *don't* feel.

Excitement. Intrigue. Amusement. Fear. Pride. Concern.

I can't help but glance at my father's expression—it's a moment I suspect I'll cherish the rest of my life. His face is red, eyes dark but wide. He's shocked—and pissed—to see her here. I hold the image in my mind for just long enough to memorize it, then I turn back.

As she marches forward, past fae shrinking back in fear, murmuring begins, and I'm reminded of her home-land. Whispers that bounce through the dark leaves of the shade maples. Of the expression on Caelynn's face as she stood in the Whisperwood for the first time in a decade. For the first time since killing my brother.

My stomach sinks as she draws close enough for me to see what's in her hand.

A head.

She carries the head of a fae swinging by its white hair, crimson blood dripping onto the marble floor of our banquet hall. Caelynn's face is impassive, her eyes harsh but glowing with golden light. Her ability to hide the brightness of her eyes long term is a talent I've not run across before. She uses emotional pain to hide her power when it suits her.

Right now, she has no desire to hide the massive amounts of magic flowing through her veins.

She's killed another fae from my court. Jasper, I recognize. He's been a guard since I was a child. That's about all I know about him, but still, it's a strange feeling.

Caelynn stares straight ahead, straight at my father who sits at the center of the feature table, right in line of the aisle. I am only feet from him, but her focus is intense, and her eyes don't waver from her target even once.

Guards charge in, feet stomping loudly—a bit delayed, I'll admit—but my father holds up his hand. He holds our intruder's gaze warily. The guards freeze, swords still held at the ready.

Her march ends only when she reaches our table and drops the dismembered head on my father's still full plate. I flinch at the squishing sound it makes as flesh meets his dinner. Blood pools, dripping onto his fork. His hooded gaze regards her, his features much more controlled than mine. I wrinkle my nose. How does he block out that putrid smell?

Caelynn leans in, three fingers pressed to the table beside the plate, her long neck stretches over the table, and her blond hair drops into the bloody mess tinging the tips of the strands in red. "Next time you send an assassin for me, make it a better one." She smiles, eyes alight with wickedness. "Oh, that's right, you sent two." Her head tilts innocently. She returns to her upright position and crosses her arms.

Sick amusement fills my belly, and I have to hold back a smirk at the spectacle. One glance down at the grey skin of the dead face on my father's plate is sobering enough to keep my wits about me.

My father's eyes narrow, but he doesn't respond. He doesn't so much as flinch—is he breathing?

"Don't underestimate me again," Caelynn says, leaning back and folding her hands behind her back casually. "Or I'll be tempted to send the next head to the High Queen and let her know what you think of her ordinances."

Caelynn's banishment was temporarily rescinded while the queen searched for a savior, someone designated to travel into fae-hell to fetch the cure for a terrible plague. As runner up, Caelynn is currently under the queen's protection. Once the cure is secured, her banishment will be reinstated.

If my father were to send assassins to the human world to kill Caelynn once this is all over with, no one would bat an eyelash, but right now? While the queen herself has declared Caelynn to be under her protection? It would end very badly for my father if it were made public.

He wrinkles his nose but otherwise doesn't speak. His eyes flit down to the head on the table for the first time.

"Yes, the other is alive," Caelynn says, as if answering the question he didn't voice. "You'll find him on edge of your iridescent forest strung up in a tree."

Caelynn turns on her heel, and my stomach sinks for the third time. Not because of what she did or who she is, but because while she was here, she never, not once, looked in my direction.

———

We watch in awe as Caelynn leaves the banquet hall. I quickly grab a napkin and use magic to scrawl a note. Then, I hand it to the wide-eyed and tense guard standing behind me. "Be sure our visitor gets this before she leaves."

The guard blinks but then nods and stands up straight, his muscles less tense than before. Apparently relieved at his new orders. Inaction tends to be a difficult task.

The moment the door shuts behind Caelynn, the room breaks into chaos with whispers and shouts. There are close to fifty royal Luminescent courtiers here for our weekend banquet. This was a larger show than I suspect Caelynn expected. Every Friday night, we invite every Lumi-fae of rank to join us for a meal. It's a weekly tradition. It's a bit pompous and annoying most of the time, but at least here, my father must keep his sharp tongue mostly to himself.

Lucky for us, despite the number of fae that witnessed Caelynn's show, the people in this room are privy to many court secrets, and it's unlikely for this one to get out.

"How did she get in here?" my father shouts.

The captain of the guard scurries to stand before my father, armor clinking erratically. His beard is long and so lacking of color it nearly blends into his shining white armor. "It's unclear, sir. She snuck by several on-duty guards. We'll conduct a thorough investigation immediately."

"I want those guards banished," my father announces.

The captain winces.

"Without a trial?" my mother whispers. She pulls at her lip anxiously.

"Caelynn is a shadow walker, Father," I say. "I imagine it would be quite easy for her to get around even our most astute guards."

"That is no excuse! She is our one and only *enemy*!"

"Clearly," I mumble, and my father shoots me a glare that could cut through ice. I raise my eyebrows, but then I sit back in my chair casually. Since I won the trials, I've earned more power and influence than I ever have before. More than my father is used to just yet. If I can manage to actually complete the quest I've been appointed, I'll be a shoo-in for the High Court. I just have to survive the Schorchedlands first.

And before that, I have to figure out how to enter the Schorchedlands—a feat much harder than assumed.

But for now, the king must accept my voice, particularly in front of the entire court. "Conduct the investigation," I tell the guard. "We will discuss their punishment in the meantime. However, you can be sure there will be no grace given if it happens a second time. Learn what you can about shadow walkers and how to use our natural abilities against shadow magic. Caelynn is particularly resourceful and powerful. Learn from this mistake and *do not* underestimate her again."

My father purses his lips, something he does when he's considering being impressed. He nods his acceptance of my command to the captain of the guard. The captain nods sharply, his shoulders less tense than only moments before. Then, he marches from the hall.

Once the whispers settle down, my father gives an impassioned speech to all in attendance. He announces that everyone in the room is duty-bound never to mention what they saw today. Together, we will defeat this *great enemy*. Yada yada.

I, however, am eager to be done with dinner, so I can talk to this *great enemy* before I miss the chance to see her again.

# 3
## CAELYNN

The guards allow me to exit through the main gates with no more than a few sneers. I simply wink and smile, playing my part. But I do realize they may have known the guard whose head I just presented to the king in an incredibly brutal manner.

If I could go back, I'd have found a more private way to make my point. Like maybe his bedroom in the middle of the night. I'd have loved to make the Luminescent Court King pee his sheets. My smile grows wider.

The patter of rushed footsteps and erratic clinking of metal alerts me to someone approaching from behind. One single guard rushes toward me, and I shift into a defensive stance, but he stops a few feet from me and simply holds out a piece of paper. Wait, no, that's a napkin.

My eyebrows pull down as I examine the napkin and unfold it.

*I hope you don't intend to leave without paying your old ally a visit.*

*Remember Raven.*

My eyebrows rise and then lower. The strange message at the bottom aside, my lips curl into a surprising smile. It seems the prince wants to see me before I leave. It's also a relief that he doesn't seem to be angry with my actions. I did kill a fae from his court, after all.

I pause to consider. I doubt I'd be welcome to just walk into the palace for a chat with the prince, even if he'd invited me.

"Thank you," I tell the guard then turn and continue my slow walk. I'd had other plans, but now, I suppose I'll have to alter those slightly. The Queen of The Whisperwood can wait one more day.

———

Getting through the gates of the Luminescent Court was surprisingly easy the second time. I don't suspect the guards considered I'd leave, just to turn back and hop back through their defenses a moment later. The guards are still reeling from the first "invasion" as I heard them call it and hardly looked up to consider a return trip.

I cover myself in shadow and slip over the white grass, sparkling like glitter dumped everywhere, then past the crystal pond and a maze made of bright white hedges. Everything here is white, scattering sunlight all around. That doesn't mean there aren't shadows, though. The open grass is nearly impossible for me to pass by without being noticed, but the hedges leave me just enough shade to blend in.

The palace itself is made of white marble, and the damn thing reflects so much light it hurts my eyes.

It's beautiful, in a typical sort of way.

I slip into a pantry window, down the hall, and up a wide set of stairs. Two guards stand in front of a familiar hall, but something about them gives me pause. Their muscles are tense, eyes darting around.

I bite my lip and consider.

I've been a spy inside this palace once before, and back then, passing through this hall was not a challenge, but that was before a shadow fae murdered one of their princes. Passing through the main gates was not a challenge either.

Would they place their most talented guards at the front gates or the most important? I purse my lips, check that my shadows are wound tightly around me, and then slink forward as quietly as possible.

In an instant, there are crossed swords blocking my path.

"Password," one of the guards says casually, looking directly at me.

My mouth falls open. Well... that's unexpected.

Password... I think back to the note. "Raven."

The swords ring as they slide apart. My eyebrows rise, and I don't dare drop my shadows as I pass them awkwardly.

I'm in front of Rev's bedroom door in only moments. I know my way around this place fairly well. I spent three full days hiding out here when I was a teenager.

The Night Bringer, an ancient being that tricked me into a terrible bargain, ordered me to assassinate a prince. If I succeeded, I'd get everything I'd ever dreamed. If I failed, I'd be his slave for eternity.

I had no choice but to comply. Except, when I'd met my mark—the fae I was sent to kill— I couldn't do it. So, I went to that ball and danced in that same banquet hall I just presented the dismembered head of a fae assassin to the king. I'd danced with the youngest heir of the Luminescent Court, not realizing who he was.

And for those few minutes, while I spun in circles beneath their glittering lights, held in his arms, I forgot my pain. My fear. My confusion. My doubt.

For those moments, I was simply a young fae dancing with a handsome boy who made me feel beautiful. Until I realized who he was.

If I hadn't figured out Rev was my fated mate, maybe I would have been able to do the deed.

Instead, I hid. I stayed hidden in the shadows of his palace for three days, searching for some escape.

I was alone and freaked out, hiding from my fate.

So, yes, I know more about this place than any outsider should.

I tap on the door.

It swings open quickly, revealing a confused Rev. His lips part in surprise.

"Caelynn." He blinks. "How did you— "

"Never underestimate a Shadow Court fae." I wink.

He knows I killed his brother in this palace, but he doesn't know how much time I spent here. He doesn't know that I spied on him too, while desperately searching for a way to save him.

I did. I found a loophole that could save his life and keep me from the Night Bringer's clutches. But it meant killing his brother in his place.

His brother was a sadistic arrogant fool that deserved his fate. I am not sorry for shoving a dagger through his chest. Because of what he threatened to do to me. Because the realm is better off without him as their king. And because by killing him, I outwitted the Night Bringer and saved Rev.

I'm proud of that kill, and no matter how much Rev loved his brother, I can't stop that from being true. I hate myself for many things, and one of them is that feeling; that sick joy swirling around inside makes me a bad person.

And that's the reason Rev and I can never be together.

I won the game, but I lost Rev. We lost our life together. Because I'm his brother's murderer, and that will never go away.

Rev lets me into his room. I shift awkwardly, crossing my arms. I bite my lips as I glance around his bedroom. It's mostly the same as a decade ago.

The desk in the corner is larger than before, more ornate. Dark mahogany instead of white, a nice contrast. There's a huge quadruple set of shelves covering the far wall full of books and a few knick-knacks. I cross the room, eyes pinned to a shoe wedged between two sets of leather-bound books.

A female's lovely black heeled boot.

My breath comes out shaky as I stare at it. Had he had it back then? I didn't notice.

I clear my throat and turn back to him. "So, how're the plans to save the world coming?" I ask him casually, trying not to show any more emotion than necessary. This place brings up memories, good and bad. Memories better left buried.

My breathing is just a tad too shallow, heart-pounding too fast.

He watches me closely. His hair has grown since the end of the trials. Black locks, slightly curled at the ends are swept to the side so they don't fall into his eyes. He's wearing a casual tunic, the sleeves rolled to his elbows exposing his intricate black thorn tattoos. His eyes are bright silver.

"Not as well as I'd have hoped." His eyes darken.

My eyebrows rise, but I shrug. "You're not dead yet. Can't be all that bad." I smirk, but it fades as I notice his expression. Something is wrong.

"It's... not good, I'll tell you that."

I purse my lips. "What is it?"

"You can't tell anyone." He lifts his shoulders in a lifeless shrug. "No mention of it. Not even to my father."

I laugh. "Your father? You're joking, right?" With any luck, I'll never even be in the same room with that man ever again.

He shrugs. "You could assume he knows and let something slip in passing. He doesn't; he doesn't know."

"Well, I'm very good with secrets." I walk past the white cushioned bench and sit on the windowsill that overlooks a small copse of white-leaved trees in the courtyard below.

"I was supposed to enter the Schorchedlands three weeks ago."

I open my mouth but stop and snap it back closed. Rev stares at the ground, his expression grim.

"Why haven't you?" I say casually, but anxiety curls in my stomach. This mission is everything. To him and the realm.

He sits on the silver sheets of his massive four-poster bed that I have very purposefully not glanced toward. His hands fall into his lap, and he stares at them. This is a very different Rev than the one I know. Confident and proud, strong and determined. This Rev almost seems... defeated.

"In order to enter the Schorchedlands," he begins slowly, "you must pass through the wall of thorns. It is impenetrable for a physical body—only bodiless souls can pass."

I nod absently. It's called "fae hell" for a reason. It is the permanent home for souls too wicked to find peace in the afterlife.

"The only exception is the Wicked Gate. The Wicked Gate is the only way in or out for anyone other than a wraith. And she will only allow one being to enter and return with their body intact every ten years."

"Yes," I prompt him to go on.

"Well, the gate refused me passage."

Rev meets my eye, the color dimming. My stomach sinks.

"Why?" I breathe. "Someone else has already passed?"

He shakes his head.

"Then, what?"

"I went three weeks ago. The queen wanted to keep the journey quiet as long as possible, knowing my time inside may be longer than the courts expect and they would get nervous. So, I went without anyone knowing. I approached the gate, slit my arm, and pressed the blood against the door. Nothing happened."

"Nothing at all?"

"It whispered to me. A message. It said, *the one who enters must belong. You cannot pass.* And then it flung me backward onto my damn butt." He sighs. "I tried three times. It stopped whispering to me and wouldn't even let me approach any longer."

I blink several times, trying to wrap my mind around it. We fought fifteen of the strongest fae, one from each court, in a brutal competition. The winner was chosen to enter the Schorchedlands in order to save us all. Inside those walls, among the souls of evil fae, is a cure to the curse plaguing our lands. But the one who won the games… cannot enter.

That's interesting. And potentially bad. Really, really bad.

If all of this was for nothing, if there's no hope for us to retrieve the cure, our world is doomed. And for Rev personally…

He needed to win the trials to prove his place in his own court or risk being outed as a bastard. His father has quietly worked to get him out of the way without his dirty business—his queen's apparent affair—coming to light. For many years, he's worked to undermine Rev's ability to rule by spreading rumors and belittling him in front of his people. Now that Rev won the trials, there's no hope such small actions could turn the people against their beloved prince.

"Do you think your father could be behind it?" I ask.

Rev blinks. "How? Why?"

"He hates that you won. He wants you to look the fool... He wants to find any reason to disinherit you."

Worse than losing the trials and his princely status, if he were to fail in his *responsibility* to save the realm... his father would have all the ammo he needs. If he cannot enter the Schorchedlands, he will be considered a failure. Everyone will blame him. Thousands of deaths will be on his hands.

He considers this, face crumpled in concentration. It's adorable, actually. "But would he really put the entire realm at risk in order to achieve it?"

I bite my lip. "Maybe he'll wait for your failure to be exposed then orchestrate a solution—I don't know, let Drake get through so he'll be the savior instead of you. It would bypass me as the runner up too."

Rev shakes his head. "That's quite a conspiracy."

I chuckle. It is. And yet I wouldn't put it past these wicked men. But I nod. "You're right, there are probably more realistic options to consider first."

I wonder if the gate does not recognize Rev as the winner of the trials. It was a fairly controversial ending. I beat our opposition and then gave the win to the magically drained Reveln because he'd sacrificed his chance to win to save Raven's life.

Perhaps, to the gate, I am the rightful savior.

That would imply some kind of magical bargain the High Court made with the gate itself, and I'm unsure if that's even possible, let alone likely. Does the gate actually care who won?

It does seem to care who enters.

My next thought is that Rev is too... pure. Too good for

that place. It is hell, after all. The message was *the one who enters must belong*. My theoretical translation: the soul of the being allowed to pass must belong in that wicked place.

Rev isn't exactly a saint, though, so even that seems outlandish.

These two theories are still problematic because, even if someone else could enter and retrieve the cure, Rev would still be considered a failure. He'd be the fae who should have saved the realm and left them to die, forcing another to save them.

"So, now what?" I say softly.

"I'm working with the queen for a solution and, well, stalling."

"Do you have any theories?"

"Some. None I like."

I bite my lip and nod. I look out the window, to the lands beyond this one. I came straight here from the human world because I wanted to give the king of the Luminescent Court a message, but I do have something quite important to do before my banishment is reinstated.

I haven't been free in the fae realm in a decade.

As a child, I had one goal. One wish. All I wanted, truly wanted, was to be a full member of the Shadow Court.

I was trapped into the Night Bringer's web before I reached even my first rite of passage. If I completed those two, I'd be invited to the Shadow Castle to meet the Queen of the Whisperwood. The castle is ancient and massive, a relic of the time our court was powerful, rather than poverty-ridden.

I'd be invited now, if only I could make my way across

the realm. I could fuel it with my magic—a gift from the very creature that destroyed my life. My pain could give the court I love life for a little while at least.

I sniff. Ironically enough, those rites of passage I was barred from as a child were two of the tasks we completed during the trials. Now, all that's left is being welcomed by the queen inside her throne room.

I've met my queen, a few times now, but never in our own court. And I still have never set foot inside my own court's palace. I long, more than anything else, to go there. To see it for myself. The history of our people. The remnants of our pride, our power that was taken from us so long ago.

I could have this one thing. It's small, and maybe even pointless. But it's something I always wanted, something I mourned during my time in the human world.

And I could have it now. All I'd have to do is leave here and go take it.

All I'd have to do is abandon Rev in his time of need.

Maybe if I'd thought it through, I wouldn't have given the win to Rev. Because if I'd won the trials, I would have been free and able to use my magic to help my poor kingdom, lift them out of obscurity, and give them hope.

But I'm not sorry. I've always picked him over me. And I'm going to do it again.

I sigh, knowing I won't be traveling to the Shadow Court any time soon. I won't enter those palace walls like I've dreamed about so many times.

Because right now, Rev needs my help. And I won't fail him.

# 4
## REV

Caelynn stares out the window for a long time, and I can't help but wonder what it is that has her so transfixed. Is she disappointed in me? Does she regret allowing me to take the victory at the end of the trials? Is she trying to puzzle it out?

After a while, I find myself just watching. Her breathing is even, calm. Her eyes dim, but not dark, not like before. Her legs long and thin, folded beneath her as she leans against the windowsill. As much as I'm not a fan of the human clothing she seems partial to, it does show off her figure. The tips of her hair are still tinged red with blood.

Finally, she turns back to me, and her eyes are noticeably darker.

What is causing her pain?

"Do you think your father will allow me to stay in the castle? Or will I have to find a home in a tree somewhere?"

"What?" I cough.

"You don't think I'd leave you when you need help, do you?" She smiles, but it doesn't reach her eyes.

I sigh. I do need her help but… "I… I can't ask that of you."

"You're not asking. I'm offering. Unless you'd rather do it on your own? I suppose I could understand that— "

"No! No, I am not that proud. I could certainly use the help. My father will definitely not allow you to stay in the castle. I don't know if you've noticed this… but he's not very fond of you."

She smiles darkly. "I don't know. The assassins were a nice parting gift."

My lips curl into a smile.

"But," she says slowly, "you do have one other ally we could call on."

My eyebrows pull down. "I'm not sure that's a good idea."

"Why not?" she asks sweetly, tilting her head. "We need someplace to hideout that isn't here. Or did you think taking on a few dozen guards per day is good training for the Schorchedlands?"

I sigh. "I don't want to tell more people about this than is necessary."

"You told me. Your sworn mortal enemy. I think you can handle requesting help from one more person."

My stomach sinks at the prospect, but it does make sense. "The Crumbling Court is the closest kingdom to the Wicked Gates in the realm." It's only thirty miles out, and I've considered calling on Tyadin before but didn't have the nerve to do it.

"Ahh. It's too bad we don't have any friends anywhere near there," Caelynn draws dramatically.

I smile, giving in to her bit, and her suggestion. "You don't suppose that dwarf friend of ours would let us in?"

Her eyes brighten, and that makes it all worth it. "Only if you promise not to call him a dwarf."

# 5
## CAELYNN

Rev insists I sleep in the spare room adjoining his for the night. This works well because I don't need to leave his room and risk gaining the guards' attention.

Tomorrow, we'll set out on our trip to the Crumbling Court.

Tonight, I am in enemy territory. In a place that holds powerful memories.

I force my mind to focus on productive things rather than those dark or selfish thoughts—like why Rev would have a spare room connected to his or about my time in this palace a decade ago.

That's an impossible task. My mind won't stop swirling with so many thoughts and memories. I'm trapped in them.

I stare up at the ivory ceiling adorned with gold swirling designs. My teeth chatter gently. I bite my lip as I think of my second favorite time in this palace. It was my second day living in the shadows of this court's palace. No one knew I was here as I desperately searched for a way out of my bargain.

And I sat in on Rev's music lesson. I was pressed to the corner, shadows covering me so thoroughly I was invisible to the fae there. He played the violin so eloquently and I closed my eyes, feeling like I could hop inside his soul and live there forever.

I open my eyes and shake my head. Even memories like those are bitter in their sweetness and laced with acid. Because I can't forget what came after.

Finally, I give up on sleep and cross the room to the window. I sit on the sill and stare out over the grounds. The view here isn't as expansive as it was in the Flicker Court. I could see for miles there, the mountains far in the distance and the desert wide open before me. It was lovely. Here, I can see a few hundred feet of Luminescent courtyards and gardens then the edge of the Iridescent Forest, and that's all. Still, it's distracting enough that the pressure on my lungs lessens as I breathe the cool air.

Soft snow begins to drift by. The Luminescent Court is quite near the Frost Court, so occasionally, their magic drifts north enough to sprinkle the lands with snow. It's quite fitting for this element. Lovely white, glistening snow. The two courts are natural allies. As is the Flicker Court for very different reasons.

A distant shout grabs my attention. My breath catches as a guard sprints towards the palace below, pointing up toward my window.

*Whoops.*

I'd let my guard down, not even thinking about someone seeing me here.

If I used shadows to cover my body, most light fae can't see me at all. But I didn't. I let my guard down and they must have seen my form sitting in the window—right next to their prince's room.

It was not far from here I killed their first prince.

I hastily fix up the bed so it doesn't look slept in, at least at first glance. Then I march into Rev's room and slip into the corner I know will remain shadowed even once lights are turned on.

If they flash their Luminescent light directly onto me, they'll see my unnaturally covered silhouette, but I'm hoping my proximity to a slumbering Rev will keep those chances low.

I don't know what will happen if I'm caught here, but it's a complication I'd rather avoid.

# 6

## REV

I jerk awake as someone busts through my bedroom door. Shouted orders and stomping boots fill the room. Before I can blink the sleep from my eyes, the room is full of guards.

"You can put the weapon down, your highness. We have it under control."

At first, I'm confused, but then I notice the dagger in my tight fist. Well, I suppose it's good those reflexes are working correctly.

"Have what under control?"

"There was an intruder seen from the window. We believe the shadow fae has infiltrated the castle."

My mouth falls open. "And did you catch the intruder?"

"Well, no, sir. Not yet. But we won't be leaving until she's found."

I roll my eyes. *Great.*

"And if she's found I'm going to have to banish the guards on gate duty."

The guard blinks back his shock, but I wave it away.

"Send Sir Simmons in, I'll have a chat with him." The Captain of the Guard will be the only person able to make the right choice here. That or my father, but he'd figure out more than I'd desire.

There are only two guards I trusted with my secret visitor.

"Yes sir." He nods to the four remaining guards stationed around my bed like it's the wall of the kingdom.

"She's obviously not in the room," I hasten to say. "Have the guards outside the doors, not caging me in like a beast."

"I'm very sorry sir, but the intruder is able to use shadow to hide from sight. We can't be too careful, at least for the time being."

I raise my eyebrows. "Learning more about shadow fae, are we?" Well, at least they took my orders seriously. I do, however, bite my tongue to keep from telling them that if they shined direct light onto potential hiding places she'd be exposed—she uses the natural darkness and shadows to her advantage. If you take away that advantage, you expose her.

But right now, it's in my best interest that they *don't* find her. And truth be told, I don't fear Caelynn. I should, I realize. She used her shadow power to hide from the guards ten years ago, slipped inside my brother's room, and...

I swallow.

If I were wise, I'd be wary of her. But apparently, I'm not wise.

She could have lied about her motives for killing Reahgan. She told me she did it to save me, and I believe her.

The magic in the trials was certainly not lying when it told me she was my fated mate. My stomach sinks at that thought.

It's a bitter truth that wedges its way into the cracks of my heart.

Maybe that's more reason I shouldn't trust her. The magic of the mating bond has a sort of hypnotizing effect. It drives me to be near her, to protect her, to care for her. And perhaps that means I'm not thinking clearly.

But it does serve one purpose: it's easier to trust someone you know is magically inclined to care for you too.

She had many chances to harm me during the trials. And given what I know, I am confident I am safe with her. My father is another story. But then again, he's not actually my father so…

It's hard to break the habit of calling him that name.

The four guards stand in a semicircle around my bed, backs facing me, ever vigilant. I flop back onto my pillow and sigh. Where is Caelynn? She was seen from the window, which means she wasn't sleeping. Is she in the halls somewhere? Or hiding in this very room?

I look around, but it's too dark to see much.

Finally, Sir Simmons marches into the room. Followed by my father.

I suppress a groan and cross my legs, still partially beneath the covers.

"You wanted to see me, Your Highness?"

"Yes," the king tilts his head, "I'm rather curious what you have to say to the guards."

*Great.* He already suspects. Oh well, let him suspect. He hates me anyway.

"I was simply going to request the guards loosen their security measures when it comes to my private sleeping quarters. The intruder is clearly not here and even if— "

"Even if what?" the king says, stepping forward, a scowl written on his face.

I keep eye contact. I'm way past backing down from this fae. "Even if she was, she is not a threat. Not to me."

Every muscle in the king's body tenses, even as he forces his expression to one of casual curiosity. "Ahhh, she's not a threat to *you.*"

I chuckle. "Relax father, I don't believe her a threat to you either."

He watches my expression closely. He wants to see if I'm lying. Fae are quite able to lie, unlike the legends humans have of us, but it is a rather uncomfortable endeavor, and it almost always shows signs. A tick or a wince or a tightened jaw.

"What other reason could she have for trespassing a third time?"

*Third?* She was here this morning but... I wince as I realize his meaning. The first time was ten years ago when she murdered my brother.

"I hadn't realized you had become such close friends." My father's words are acid, and I narrow my eyes.

"Allies, Father."

"So, you do not care for her?"

I consider responding, but there is no correct response. And to be honest, I'm not sure what is lie and what is truth when it comes to her. Would I flinch if I were to tell my father I don't care for her? She's... God, I have no idea what she is.

So, I decide not to respond at all.

"I have intentions on making a trip to the Crumbling Court first thing in the morning. I will be out of your hair then."

The king's lip curls in disgust. He steps forward, a menacing expression on his face, and for the first time in my life, I wonder if my father would try to kill me. I wonder what the guards might do if he attacked me. Would they defend me or follow his orders? He leans over my bed, eyes full of dark hatred. "You are no son of mine," he whispers.

Sir Simmons winces. I clench my jaw. "I'm aware."

He blinks away his instant of surprise, and anger returns to his controlled expression. He stands up straight, eyes cast past me to the corner of the room. "If I find that whore in my palace again, I'll remove her head from her body myself. And I'll do it slowly. Damn the consequences from the High Court." With another curl of his lip, he whispers, "The Night Bringer sends his regards." With obvious effort, he forces his body to spin, and he stomps from my room, slamming the door behind him.

Sir Simmons pauses, glancing back to me. "Are you all right, Your Highness?"

"Perfectly well, thank you." I force a smile. "I appreciate your diligence, but your guards are no longer needed. You can call off the search as well."

He purses his lips, his expression unreadable. Then, he nods and calls the guards to follow him.

Once the door closes, I let out one long breath.

# 7
## CAELYNN

My heart pounds so hard it's hard to hear much beyond the pumping pulse in my ears. Finally, the last guard leaves the room, and I let out a breath and drop the shadows from around me.

"Have I ever mentioned your father is a dick?" I say with a weak voice.

Rev whips around to look at me and blinks. I wasn't sure if he'd known I was there or not. "He's not my father," he says simply.

"Yeah. I know." I take in a few more deep breaths then sit on the edge of his bed. "He looked right at me. He knew I was here." I can't bring myself to mention his comment. I can't say his name. Not aloud.

Rev swallows, the look in his eye tells me he agrees. "But if he knew, why didn't he— "

"I don't know," I say. "He could have called me an intruder and had me arrested."

"Perhaps he knew I'd defend you to the queen. And if I

did that, you may give proof of the assassins. Did you really leave the other assassin alive?"

"Yes," I whisper. "I don't kill excessively."

"I don't know that would have been excessive. Justified, more likely."

"I got my point across with one head. I didn't need two." I only took that head because the fae was already dead. I'd stabbed him through the heart during our skirmish. The other knew he was beat and surrendered. No need to tell all of that to Rev, though.

"We really must get out of here at first light now. They'll be looking for you, and I wouldn't take my father's threat lightly."

I nod. "I wouldn't dream of it."

"You should try to get some sleep," Rev says softly. "Would you like to take the bed? I can sleep on the sofa."

"No!" I say quickly. "I wouldn't dream of tossing a prince from his bed." I chuckle, secretly hoping my cheeks aren't visibly red. "I can take the sofa."

"You weren't sleeping. That's why they noticed you."

I nod. "A stupid mistake. It won't happen again."

Rev sighs. "Anything the matter?"

*Everything*, I think. So much. "No, nothing especially. It's just strange being here."

He nods absently.

"Before we leave tomorrow," I say, mostly out of a desire to change the subject. "You should go to the library and grab any books on the Schorchedlands you can find."

His eyebrows flick up then down. "I've read as much as I could already—you're not the only one with a love for history."

I smile. To be honest, I don't even remember telling him I love history. I must have mentioned it during the trials. "I'd like to bring them with us. I don't suspect the Crumbling Court will have as many resources as you do."

He nods slowly. "I'll deal with it in the morning. It's time for sleep."

"Okay," I whisper.

He lays back, and I walk slowly to the couch on the other side of the room.

"Caelynn?" Rev whispers.

"Yes?" I squeak. *How pathetic is that?*

"Are you all right?"

"Yeah, I'm fine," I say, knowing I'm too far and the room is too dark for him to see me flinch as my gut clenches.

Truth? No. Not at all. For so many reasons.

# 8

## REV

When I wake in the morning, the sun is already bright and intrusive. Caelynn is nowhere to be found. But then again, maybe I just can't see her.

I focus, casting my gaze around the room, testing to see if I could break through her shadow magic illusion. I don't even know for sure if she's still in the room—but it seems unlikely she'd take the chance of running about the grounds after nearly being caught last night.

I examine every corner of the room where there is even remote shade—nothing. Disappointed, I take in a big breath. "Caelynn?" I ask, defeat a bitter taste in my mouth.

No response.

I purse my lips. Maybe she isn't here after all.

I roll out of bed and find a note sitting on the table by the window. I unfold the paper and read the few words scrawled on the parchment:

. . .

***Meet me in the forest. Don't forget the books.***

I sigh and begin packing up immediately, wondering why she left before me. She could have woken me if she was eager to get moving. It's strange to have her helping me, to be honest. I'm partially relieved to have an ally, someone to trust.

Another part of me knows I'm insane because that person is Caelynn from the Shadow Court.

I shake my head. She ruined her life to save mine a decade ago. She was forced into that bargain. There's still a lot I don't know about the shadow fae, but I do believe her when she said she hates herself for what she did.

Over on my desk, I grab the three books I'd been scouring through most recently. There are another four in the library I'll grab before leaving. I'd read through those thoroughly already, but maybe Caelynn will see something I hadn't. Or Tyadin. Maybe we'll get new information that paired with old, and we can come up with a plan.

I hold on to that vague hope.

Because right now, based on everything I know, I'm totally screwed.

# 9
## CAELYNN

I find a spot on a low hanging branch of a white maple near the path, and I settle in for a long wait. My fingers glide over the oddly smooth bark. This tree won't scratch my legs the way the one outside Raven's dorm did.

My stomach sinks at that thought. What's Raven doing now? Is she angry or sad or... just fine? She'll be starting classes tomorrow. She was so excited to start at that new school, where no one knew she was a foster kid or about her drug-addicted mother.

I hope she loves it. I hope so much for her it hurts.

Above me, through the nearly see-through glimmering leaves, the sun is making its slow trek into the sky. I sniff, as I watch it with a heavy heart.

My magic rumbles within my veins, aching for movement. *Yeah, yeah, I know this is boring, but we have to wait for Rev,* I think to it like it has a mind of its own. I mean, maybe it does. It did once before. I'm reminded of the time it was an external power, living inside of me, whispering in my ear. *Kill.*

Does it still desire destruction and spilled blood? Based on its origin, I wouldn't be surprised. That creature desired pain, power, and control in any way he could obtain it.

The magic is mine to rule now, but sometimes I feel *him.* The Night Bringer gave me this magic. It's part of him.

He hasn't used it to hunt me down, though I suspect he could if he wanted. So, what? Has he given up on me and moved on to some other plaything? Or is he waiting?

Or maybe, maybe I'm still playing his games without realizing it.

# 10

## REV

I can feel my father's eyes on me as I prepare my steed for departure. He's on his balcony, high on the fourth floor, just watching. Guards flank the pathway into the forest, all on high alert.

I prepare to mount my stag, Killian: a lovely golden offspring of my brother's chosen heir gift. A stag he never even rode before his death. His coat is a shiny bronze, and his antlers large and glistening like true gold.

I clear my throat, pushing those thoughts from my mind and readjust the saddle, followed by the stirrups. Never mind that my brother would hate me if he knew I'd befriended his murderer. Well, actually, Reahgan was all about power. He might be annoyed with me for my chosen allies, but he'd recognize the logic. Caelynn is powerful, she's smart and she's loyal.

*She's a means to an end*, I tell myself.

Once I get the cure, her banishment will be reinstated, and it will all be moot anyway. I can still do this. I can still secure all of the things I desire.

I'll never have a true mate, but that's something I can live with. Caelynn can go back to her human lover, I'll make sure my father leaves her be, and I'll be king.

That's that.

A gentle sparkle catches my attention on the side of the stone pathway. A little rebellious Lumistone bush has sprouted like a weed in a place it's most certainly not supposed to be. My mother will certainly rip it out the first moment she sees it.

These plants have purplish-grey vines that wind and twist up and around anything they come into contact with; they'll overwhelm structures if they're not stopped. We have a garden shed on the north side of the grounds completely covered in them and a few trellises decorating the side of the gates.

They grow a fruit specific to my court that looks a bit like a small white grape, but if you cup it in your hand, it will reflect a rainbow of colors, scattering over your fingers gently. The fruit remains juicy and sweet on the vine but is only edible for a few minutes once plucked. They begin drying quickly, and after six months, they become stone-like. They're not valued in our magical currency system, but they're quite lovely and cherished by only this court.

I pluck one of the tiny fruits, stare at it for entirely too long. Then, I slip it into my pocket as a sign of what will never be.

I take in a long breath, banishing the ache in my chest. What I would do if things were different... well, I don't even need to dwell on it. Because what's done cannot be undone.

I swallow, mount my stag, and send one last fleeting

glance to my father who watches me with clear condemnation. *Don't worry, father,* I think, giving him a sharp nod in fair well, *I'll never give you the chance to disown me. You'll live the rest of your life knowing a bastard child, not even your own blood, is the only legacy you leave behind.*

It's that thought that has a smile curling my lips, and I spur my stag into action, galloping through the gates of a palace I was never meant to inherit.

But I will take it, regardless. A weed like the Lumistone plants. He didn't rip me out by the root while he had the chance and now—I'm not going anywhere.

My stag gallops down the pathway through the Iridescent Forest—white oaks whose leaves are near see-through, casting off light from the sun and scattering it all around like a forest of mirrors. As children, we used to gather piles of leaves and then maneuver them so that the light projected a pattern or image, like constellations. Or we'd create mazes and try to crawl through without touching a ray of light.

This forest holds a host of memories. I know it like it's my own home. So, when a whisper of magic tickles my ear, I pull my stag to a complete stop. His hooves skid on the ground, pebbles flying.

Another indistinguishable whisper sounds from a path to the west. It bounces around, calling to me. Then, there's another. And another. A whispering tone I recognize but can't understand. The feeling shifts through me, delving deep into my soul.

I smile and direct Killian down the west trail, following the magic until finally, I spy the shadow fae sitting on a branch of a white maple, smiling at me.

"Took you long enough," she says, her tone light.

"You didn't need to leave the palace so early. It's not my fault you decided to sleep in a damn tree."

She hops to the ground, wiping her hands on her pants. "I figured it would be easier to get out of there while it was still dark." She shrugs. "Nice stag." She rubs his nose gently.

"Thanks."

"Do you need him? I thought you said there was a portal nearby?"

I nod. "It's about five miles off. Not far, but it will take us near the gates. It'll be another thirty miles or more to reach the Crumbling Court stronghold."

She purses her lips, an odd expression on her face.

"I couldn't get a stag for you without being unnecessarily obvious. My father might already know we're working together, but my people don't."

Her smile is bitter, eyes dark. "I understand."

"You are welcome to join me. There is plenty of room for two."

Her eyebrows rise, her lips curl into a smile I can't take my eyes off of. "Your stag is not faster than I am."

"Oh!" I match her smile with one of my own. "You think you can keep up, do you?" Excitement already pumps through my body. I do love a challenge, almost as much as I love being right.

"Try me."

Without missing another beat, I kick my stag into action and press him into a full sprint, adrenaline pumping, eyes focused. Trees blur by as we soar through the forest, my stag's stamp light and agile. Fae are fast, but a war mount like Killian will always be faster. No exceptions. And yet I hold nothing back. The trek is only a few miles, so even if my victory is extreme, I'll be able to backtrack and find her easily.

And I know she'll give it her all, so I give mine.

I round the bend, the trees thinning, and I see the marble archway where the path dead ends. I continue pressing Killian on as if my competition could be anywhere near me. As if she were next to me, challenging my win.

I pull Killian to a skidding stop but before we complete our halt, a shadow shifts and reveals an incredibly beautiful blond fae, leaning against the arch and smiling wickedly.

I cannot even explain the things that smile does to me. My bones melt, mind frozen, heart pattering. Tongue tied.

"How?" I finally get out.

She beat me. She somehow won this race, and I've never seen someone look more beautiful while doing it.

She chuckles darkly. "Just when I thought you'd learned to stop underestimating me."

I raise my eyebrows. "Never, apparently."

"I'm a shadow walker, remember?"

An inky black mist envelopes her, and an instant later she's standing beside Killian. He rears back, shuffling and huffing uncomfortably, but Caelynn mumbles softly to calm him until he allows her to rub his nose.

"You can leap through shadows?"

"Something like that."

"How far?"

"A few dozen feet at a time."

I blink slowly. Wow. It's not as good as the mile I was imagining but still rather impressive.

"It requires magic, so I don't often use the ability if I can help it."

I nod. It's always best to conserve energy when possible. I hop off of Killian and adjust his reins, patting his neck. Then, I lead him forward, toward the arch.

He huffs again, jerking his head.

"Not a fan of portals, huh?"

I shake my head. "Most animals aren't. Feels unnatural to them, I suppose."

Caelynn nods.

I circle Killian around to give me enough distance to lead him into a trot just before we reach the portal. He resists the moment the sizzle of magic becomes audible, but the bit of speed we built allows me to pull him through without much hassle. He stamps and huffs several more times once we are firmly on the other side—a good six hundred miles away from the Luminescent Court. The trees are darker, the leaves deep green, bark thick and heavy almost as if made of stone.

Caelynn takes in a long breath the moment she stops beside us in this new land. Does she feel closer to home here? The Crumbling Court is less than a hundred miles south east of her homeland in the Shadow Court. That's still a ways away, of course, but it's one of the closest courts to hers.

The queen set up this portal specifically for me and my quest shortly after the games ended. It puts us only about five miles north of the Schorchedland gates. It allowed me to do some work understanding this place, especially once I realized it wouldn't allow me to pass through.

Over the green forest, the very top of the massive wall made entirely of green vines covered in sharp thorns can be seen. It makes me sweat just being this close. I don't fear the cursed lands or the dangers trapped inside. It's the threat of inevitable failure that looms over me.

Ever since Caelynn brought up the idea of my father sabotaging me, I haven't been able to stop that thought from taking root in my mind. But I'd already scoured the place, up and down the vine walls, looking for signs of some kind of unnatural curse or recent charms. There's really not much of anything. Remnants of wraith bargains, but that's fairly standard and couldn't possibly have anything to do with my particular struggle.

If I cannot get inside those walls... I will forever be remembered as a failure. I will be hated. And the death of every fae in the land will be on my head. I swallow and bite the inside of my lip.

My only saving grace right now is that there has been a lull in the curse's movement. It isn't actively prowling through our lands at the moment. The scourge—a plague turning everything it touches into stark decay and sucking the ground of its magic entirely—hasn't spread in weeks.

The queen has kept me mostly updated on its progress. Right now, she's not breathing down my neck to figure my shit out because her people are not actively dying. That will change soon, and I'll know I've run out of time.

"We'll find a way," Caelynn promises, her voice soft and comforting. I've heard her voice dark and menacing, stubborn and fiery. But it's this tone that affects me the most. It sends a shudder all the way through me.

We walk down the uneven path, leading away from the Wicked Gates, and with each step, the pressure eases.

After pushing Killian hard in my pathetic loss, I allow him to take a leisurely pace without my weight holding him down.

The first mile takes an achingly long time, though part of me enjoys the relaxation. The calm forest and lack of urgency. Something about Caelynn sets me at ease. Which is incredibly ironic considering she shoved an obsidian blade through my brother's heart a decade ago.

I'm not sure why I insist on reminding myself of that fact so frequently. Perhaps it's because I need the reminder. I need it so that I'll remember to stop staring at her slender figure. Or dwelling on her impressive power and hypnotic smile.

Finally, I hop back onto Killian. No need to develop sore feet this soon into my journey. Besides, I brought that damn stag for a reason; I may as well ride him.

Once settled on the saddle, I hold my hand out for Caelynn.

"Hell no."

I purse my lips and consider arguing with her. But I know better.

I canter with Killian for two additional miles, Caelynn keeping up easily, but her gait is awkward. Over time a legitimate limp shows more and more. Finally, I notice her hand fall to her thigh and come away slick with blood.

I pull Killian to a stop immediately. "When did you do that?"

She shrugs, continuing a quick march.

"Caelynn."

"I injured it during the fight with the assassins. It must have reopened during our race. It's fine."

"Get on the damn stag," I tell her.

She clears her throat, her jaw clenches tight, her arms crossed.

I shake my head and hop onto the ground. "Fine. You ride, I'll run."

"I'm not taking your stag from you."

"Well, I'm not letting you continue on in pain. So, ride with me, or we'll make camp here for the night."

"It's not even *noon.*" She holds her palms out in annoyance.

"Then, it will be a long-ass night."

"You're so stubborn."

"You're *joking.*" I blink. She thinks I'm the stubborn one?

She smirks but then rolls her eyes. "Fine! I'll ride the damn stag. The injury isn't anything to worry about, though."

"No reason to stress it." It does cross my mind that I could heal it. But healing is such an *intimate* thing—my magic, my essence, enters the body, stitching the fae up from the inside out—that I'm not sure I want to do that with Caelynn a second time.

The first time, I hated her. I couldn't understand my drive to protect her, her hold over me. But now, I know the why, and somehow that makes it worse.

She's my fated mate.

She's the partner my magic chose for me. I hardly even

know what that means, but that makes it all the scarier. Especially with someone I know I can never truly be with, for many reasons.

So, now that I know—now that I've forgiven her for the unforgivable act of killing my brother—I don't know if I could let myself become that vulnerable with her again. Even if it's just a shallow leg injury.

I hop back onto Killian easily and hold my hand out for her. She takes it without meeting my eye and leaps up onto the saddle behind me.

She attempts to sit far back on Killian's rear, but the saddle dips and as soon as we begin moving, she slips closer and closer to me. Her chest presses to my back in only moments. Her annoyed grunt makes me chuckle.

She reluctantly rests her hand on my waist, and my heart stutters a beat. Her body heat sears my skin.

"Is this okay?" she whispers.

"Yes," I say with an easy chuckle that isn't at all a representation of the level of ease inside my body. I'm wound like a top, ready to explode.

Caelynn and I spent a lot of time together during the trials, but in all of that, despite becoming extremely vulnerable, we were rarely this close physically. We never touched, not if we could help it.

*She's not going to stay*, I remind myself.

My conflicting feelings for her don't matter. I can't be attracted to her; I'm not allowed to want her. Because, with any luck, in a matter of days, I'll be inside the Schorchedlands, and when I return, she'll be sent right back to the human world.

It won't matter. So long as I don't let myself get too entangled in her.

The future our magic intended for us can never come to pass. It's up to us how much that fact shatters us in the process.

# 11

## CAELYNN

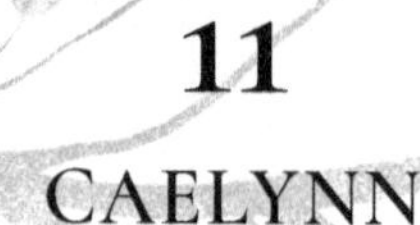

My hands rest gently on Rev's waist, and I torture myself, running through every place our bodies are currently touching. On every feeling, every shift of our bodies. The way we move together with the rhythm of this beautiful stag's clomping hooves.

Stupid mind. Stupid body. Stupid magic.

Prince Reveln of the Luminescent Court might need my help. He might even trust me. But he won't ever want me. And even if he does, what difference does it make? I'm doomed. My future set.

Whatever might have been, the residual feelings between us will be snuffed out soon enough.

Rev's muscles are tense; I can tell because my body is flush against his.

"What you thinking about?" I ask casually.

He clears his throat, shoulders straightening. "Nothing."

I snort. Perhaps he feels uncomfortable about our

closeness because he dislikes it. I bite my lip and shift away from him. I don't get very far. This saddle isn't made for two people.

The stag clomps through the lush green forest, right on the edge of a stony mountain range. These are the mountains our friend Tyadin spent basically all of his childhood. As half-dwarf, he's short, stocky, and hairy, and he has an affinity for stone. It's his magical element as well, which came in handy as our ally during the trials.

He's likely the only other person in this entire magical world I trust. And to be honest, that trust only goes so far, even with Rev.

*Raven.* Raven, I trust entirely. But she's in a whole different world now.

I let out a long breath, allowing myself to miss her. She was my light during my banishment to the human world. She was the only person to ever give me hope.

I know I was bad for her, but I can't help but miss the way she looked at me. Like I was something prized. Something precious. Something to be cherished.

Never, not in my entire life, has anyone ever looked at me that way.

And I used her because I couldn't bear to give it up. It almost got her killed.

Oh, actually no, it *did* get her killed. Rev just happened to bring her back to life, despite not even knowing who she was. He knew I cared, and he acted.

"What are you thinking about?" Rev asks.

I hold my breath for a moment. "Raven," I breathe.

His shoulders tense. "Oh," he says. "How is she?" His

voice is low and slow. Like he's being careful with his words. Like I'm an animal he may spook.

"I'm not sure. Safe, I think. That's what matters."

"Is… that what you were thinking about?" he asks, but I'm quiet for probably too long.

I'm not sure what he thinks about Raven. Our relationship was… complicated. "No. I was just thinking that I miss her. That I trust her."

"You don't trust me?"

"I do. But in a different sort of way."

He nods slowly. "This part is going to get rocky," he says, and at first, I think he's talking about us or this conversation, but then I notice that we are turning onto a trail leading up into a rocky summit.

"Can Killian make it up that?"

"He was bred to be able to climb mountains. I chose him for a reason."

I decide not to comment on that because anything I'd say would make me sound very ignorant. So, Rev has multiple steeds to choose from, does he? I hadn't even thought about stags, or horses, or whatever other creatures fae use to travel on, to begin with. My family didn't have mounts. We didn't even have a bathroom inside our home.

Rev and I lived very different lives.

I am still technically fae royalty. I'm a countess—or I was before I was banished and disinherited. But in a court as poor as mine, being a count or countess is meaningless because we didn't have the magical power to fuel an estate as elaborate as the one we owned. Instead, we left it to fall apart and lived in a small cottage in a little village near the Whisperwood.

Ironically, I could fuel that estate easily now. I could fuel the palace and much of the kingdom with the power the Night Bringer granted me. And earning that power got me banished from this world entirely.

Killian clomps up the mountain as Rev and I rock and sway awkwardly. I grip his waist tighter, and his hand falls to my knee, steadying me.

Now, my heart pounds for another reason.

We climb a few hundred feet before the path evens out and our vision clears from indistinguishable rock walls to a huge valley and a castle set in between two mountains. I wouldn't have ever found this place on my own.

The castle isn't overly large, but it does appear quite luxurious from what I can see. It is made of smooth grey stone with white marble braided into the pattern. A lovely mixture of dark and light. A symbol of the fae and dwarf alliance this court is known for, perhaps? The spires reach up high, each with a winged gargoyle guarding it.

I find myself wondering if they're simple decoration or real creatures that come to life when the moon rises. Either is possible. Gargoyles are very much real, but their likeness is also imitated often enough.

We reach a wide cavern with one narrow line of stone crossing it and a short, stalky guard in full armor blocking it. That can't possibly be a bridge, could it? We slow to a casual walk as we approach the guard.

"State your name and purpose!" his voice booms before we reach him.

Rev pulls his stag to a stop still a dozen feet away. "Prince Reveln of the Luminescent Court. I am here to see Tyadin Ironhammer. I believe he's expecting me."

The guard's eyes narrow, and he lifts his chin. "Password."

"Orb of Terrors."

I blink as the guard steps aside. "Why the Orb of Terrors? And I hadn't realized he was expecting us."

Rev doesn't respond immediately and urges his mount ahead.

I hop from the stag before we pass over the narrow passage because I trust my own balance way more than Rev's golden war stag.

"Scared?" Rev teases.

"Ha ha." Also, hell yeah, I am.

When we're nearly halfway across the bridge, he finally answers my question. "He isn't specifically expecting us. Not now, at least. But he'd offered his help and gave me the password the last time we spoke. He told me it would be his least favorite part of the trials."

"Why not the best?"

"Too easily guessed." Rev shrugs.

Once across the passage, we continue down another winding trail that leads to a tunnel with huge and elaborate archways of braided stone. Shadows overtake us as we enter into the mouth of the lovely cave, and a wonderful smell of something like lavender overtakes me.

"Wow," I breathe.

I bump into Killian's rear. "Dude!"

"Sorry, can't see much. It's dark."

I chuckle. "Oh, sweet luminescent child." I slip past the stag and his rider, pressing my back to the cool stone. Then, I grip Killian's reigns and guide him forward while uttering soothing words.

Finally, we reach an entryway, the ceiling is domed and torches light the whole room. I don't even get a moment to examine it all before a voice booms through the whole place. "Hadn't thought I'd see you again, *shadow fae.*"

I flinch until I turn and see a familiar dwarfish fae smiling at me.

"Hello, Tyadin."

# 12

## REV

"I wasn't sure you'd ever make it up here," Ty says. "I was on my way out for a hike in the mountains, but I suppose I'll have to rearrange my schedule now." He laughs easily and waves us over.

I decide to leave out that the visit was Caelynn's idea.

Tyadin fetches a stable hand to take Killian to the stables, and then he ushers us through another dark tunnel. It twists and turns, the darkness is overwhelming. I am used to my brightly lit court where everything is visible. Here, it's dark and winding. You never know what's around the next corner. The torches lighting the pathways are so far apart it leaves us in darkness much more often than I'd prefer.

I suppose this is more Caelynn's element, though. I'd be curious to examine her expression... but it's too dark to see it.

Finally, we reach what appears to be the entrance to the castle. There are a set of doors thirty feet high, rustic wood, and steel braced. Opposite the doors is a grand staircase, which means we're already inside the castle. We went a back way?

We pass a pair of lanky fae whispering in the corridor and keep moving without a word to them. Down a smaller hall and through a wooden door, we enter a sitting room with a roaring fire and stained glass windows. There are two sets of bookshelves on one side of the room, and the rest are decorated with old portraits of fae I couldn't name. The floor is grey stone, but there is a large red area rug that's thick and warm.

"Swanky digs, Tyadin," Caelynn says, examining a case full of trinkets.

"What?" Ty asks.

"Nice place," she amends with a chuckle.

"Oh, thanks. It's a pretty big change for me. I just moved here after the trials. I spent most of my life in the mountains with my father. My mother grew up here, though." His mother is full fae, his father's full dwarf. He likely lived a very different life even just months ago than he is now.

"How did you get chosen as champion? I don't think you ever told us," Caelynn asks, as she plops down on one of the dark fur couches.

"The council held a trial of our own, just a simple dueling tournament. The winner was our representative in the trials. It didn't matter that my father was a dwarf or that I don't look even remotely fae because the only prerequisite to entering was being a citizen of the Crumbling Court. I think the queen was pleased a dwarfish fae won because it's a good representation of who we are as a court. My competition was low, though. Even with an open tournament, there were only seven entrants. I think many fae were afraid of having to compete with the ruling courts. There was a lot of pressure for us to prove ourselves."

"They were proud of you, I'm guessing." Caelynn smiles.

"Very. Even though I basically dropped out of the trials. I could have completed that orb challenge, I just... didn't think it was worth it anymore."

I swallow and look down at my feet.

"But I made it pretty far. Made allies. They were more than happy with my performance. Honestly, if I'd failed in the second trial, I think they would have been happy. The shadow-vyrn story is legendary around here."

Caelynn laughs.

"I'd say you should be prepared to sign a few autographs during your stay here, but the whole court is a bit distracted at the moment."

"Why, what's going on?"

"Uh, well, it's dwarfish stuff, actually. Nearly half of this court has some amount of dwarfish blood, so the rightful heir to the dwarfish throne showing up out of nowhere—well, it's pretty big news." Tyadin's eyes glisten, the amber color shinning more than usual. And I know immediately this news means a lot to him.

"A dwarfish king? One of the lost heirs?" Caelynn asks.

Tyadin told us the whole story of the dwarfish people's fall a century ago. It's not a story fae among the ruling courts know very well. Bits and pieces, sure, but Tyadin gave us a perspective only a dwarf could give.

Basically, the king was killed by an ancient beast, and

his two sons were taken by conflicting factions, both claiming they had the rightful heir to the throne. This resulted in a civil war, followed by a goblin invasion, and well, that was the end of the dwarfish kingdom. They're scattered across the realm now, having no real place to call home.

Tyadin nods and runs his fingers through his long black hair. "It's well documented that one of the heirs died. So, if he is really the other... he's indisputably the true dwarf king now."

Tyadin is quiet for a while, looking at his boots.

"So, what does that mean, exactly?" I ask. Wondering, mostly, what this means for my friend. I know he is very proud of his dwarfish heritage, so will he go following after this king? Assuming I believed his story, that's what I would do in Ty's shoes. "Is this heir going to rally the dwarves to follow him?"

"He says he wants to reclaim his throne in the old mountains. He's putting together a group of dwarves willing to fight with him. I don't think he'll get many followers but..."

Caelynn's eyes narrow.

"But you're going," I say definitively, the expression on his face and the shy yet proud stance illustrate his feelings on the matter fairly well.

He nods. "It's probably a fool's errand. The chances that a small group of dwarf warriors could chase out the goblins, defeat whatever fell creature still lurks in those mountains, and rebuild the kingdom..."

"You'll probably die trying," I agree.

"Thanks." He rolls his eyes and throws a pillow at my

head. I catch it easily and then lean over the back of the couch.

"But if it was me," I continue, "I'd rather die fighting for my dreams than live with regret and wonder *what if*."

Tyadin smiles. "Thanks." He takes a seat across from Caelynn, who, I notice, is staring at me. I meet her gaze, wondering what she's thinking, but she immediately blinks and turns away.

Tyadin clears his throat. "So, Caelynn, I'm surprised to see you here. How did you hook back up with Rev?"

Caelynn blinks, her eyes wide, but she recovers quickly. "Well, that's an interesting story."

"She had a delivery for my father," I tell him simply.

"Oh?"

"An assassin's head."

Tyadin smacks his hand over his eyes. "You didn't."

"I did," she says, not at all bashful.

I laugh. "It was pretty badass actually. It came as a surprise, but the look on my father's face when she came marching into our banquet hall—I swear, I'll cherish that moment the rest of my life."

"Damn, sounds like I missed an iconic moment."

"You did."

"So, I assume you're here because you need help with your mission. What is it you need?"

I take in a long, awkward breath and then force myself to say the words. I recount to Tyadin my failed attempt at getting through the Wicked Gates, and immediately, the countenance in the room changes. Tyadin leans forward, eyes focused on nothing at all as he listens intently. He's taking this seriously, and already some of the tension between my shoulders eases.

I'm not alone anymore. I have allies.

We're not any closer to a solution, but I know I have his and Caelynn's full efforts to aid me.

"So, our goal," Caelynn says, "is to get him through those gates, by whatever means necessary."

"We could catapult him over?" Ty muses, a sly grin spreading on his face.

"Ha ha." Caelynn rolls her eyes

"Seriously, I would do it if it'd work." I swallow, my expression still serious despite their jokes. "I don't care if I get back out again... I have to get *in* and get that cure."

"Well, you need to get back *out* or the cure won't come with you," Tyadin says.

"Whatever, you know what I mean. I can't be remembered as a failure, rejected by even the Wicked Gates."

"It could be a good thing," Tyadin muses. "You were rejected for being too pure? That wouldn't be such a bad legacy, would it?"

"Sure, I'll be just good enough to fail the entire realm and allow thousands to die. No one will care *why* I failed, they'll only know that I did. And also, no, that isn't the issue. You don't have to be a murderer—" I pause, forcing my eyes not to dart to Caelynn. She's noticeably still as I fight my brain to find the words to continue. "You don't have to be evil to go in. Historically, there are many counts of people going in and coming out that are heroes of their times even before they enter."

"But that doesn't mean they don't have their demons," Caelynn says.

"And I have them too." If she could only feel the anger swirling through my chest now. My selfish pursuit of power. My hatred for my own... I shake my head. He's not my father. "I'm telling you, it is not because I am too *pure*."

"Well, theory number two," Tyadin says, expression still stone serious as he concentrates, "is it possible the gates don't recognize you as the winner of the trials?"

Rev sniffs. "I asked the queen this—it was an awkward conversation, but it had to be done. She said there was no particular reason the gate would care about the trials at all. Anyone could enter."

"Well, sounds like the queen is a lot of help," Caelynn mumbles. "Any other theories?"

"Nothing promising. The gate is just being a dick and will change its mind if I keep trying? The sorcerer who started the scourge also put a curse on it so that no one can enter? That it's actually a riddle I need to solve?" I shrug.

"Well, let's keep trying then," Caelynn says confidently. "We'll make a trip to the gates tomorrow. You'll try, and we'll be witnesses—see if we notice something you don't. Best case, you get through tomorrow, and you're on your way to being the savior of the realm. Worst, we're back to where we were, and we'll brainstorm again after."

I take in a long breath and nod. It does feel good to have a plan, as simple as it is. There's a step ahead; even though I already know how it will end, it's still comforting.

# 13
## CAELYNN

Tyadin presents us with guest rooms right next to each other. His apartment is two floors above ours, but he spends several hours in Rev's room. Long enough that he either sleeps there or I simply never hear him leave.

I flip through the books Rev provided, learning as much about the Wicked Gates as possible. It feels like such a masochist endeavor. I've known that my soul is bound for the Schorchedlands when I die for a full decade. It's a fate I can't avoid after everything I've done. My soul has been tattered and scarred since the day I wandered into the wrong tunnel inside the Cave of Mysteries ten years ago—the moment the Night Bringer shoved his talon through my chest. Or perhaps it was when I agreed to his bargain and his magic entered my body. Either way, the girl who entered those caves did not come out.

So, learning details about the fae afterlife and the broken souls bound to it isn't my favorite research subject. *It's all to help Rev*, I remind myself. I want his life to be worth sacrificing mine for. I want to know I made the right choice.

I heave in a long breath through my nose and continue reading.

There are three distinct sections of the Schorchedlands. The outer edge, the inner circle, and finally, the core. Each section holds worse and worse evil spirits. Each inch closer to the center, it becomes hotter, the world darker, the smog thicker. Living beings can't survive for more than a few hours inside the core because the air is poisonous to them.

One of Rev's books tells the tale of twelve fae who had entered through the Wicked Gates and returned. One of them lived an entire year inside the walls. Another of his books is about the legends surrounding the origin of the Schorchedlands. The beings that created the fae realm and its people had infighting between them, and three of those ancient beings created a magical place of punishment, so strong that even one of their own would be trapped once bound to the place. I graze through that book, but the story reminds me so much of the Night Bringer that I can't bring myself to focus too heavily on it. If the Schorchedlands holds a being like him—or perhaps worse—I certainly don't want to know about it.

The Wicked Gate, it reads, was spelled to only allow one living being to enter and return every ten years. The return part being key.

Living beings can enter as much as they would like, but with the clear understanding that they can never return. Any living being who enters must give the Wicked Gate a formal request of total free will. The purpose was so that no one could be coerced into the lands as mortal punishment.

The book says nothing about a prerequisite for getting into the realm. It says nothing about needing to answer a riddle or needing to have a tarnished soul.

It does, however, explain that in addition to the initial purpose of holding the most evil of powerful beings, it was always intended to be a temporary holding. That every soul is redeemable, no matter how sullied, and once any soul within achieves the redemption they missed while in the land of the living, they will then pass onto the next life.

This is the reason many wraiths accept bargains from the living. Some just for a sense of adventure, for a chance to cause mischief in the world they once inhabited, but for others, it's a chance to redeem what they missed while living.

*Souls needn't be entirely pure to pass on,* the book says. *Many souls have several conflicts weighing them down. But one negative attribute will stand out most significantly. Your gravest sin. Your deepest seeded flaw.*

*This becomes the soul's new quest. Resolve it, and be redeemed. Refuse, and remain forever.*

*The Schorchedlands exist to hold evil spirits away from the living but also to allow these spirits the opportunity to face their single most damaging flaws and fix them. Once this single quest is completed, they will be expelled from the land of death and given life anew.*

The text then goes on to list the most common solutions to an unredeemed soul.

Selflessness. Humility. Forgiveness—themselves or others. Acceptance. Truth. Honest caring.

They're fairly vague answers that don't tell me much. Beneath each is an example of a soul who was redeemed by one of those things.

I must fall asleep somewhere in this list because the next thing I know, someone is knocking on my door hollering from the hallway.

"Shut up, Tyadin!" I grumble, pulling my face out of the parchment. My hair sticks oddly to the side of my face. *Great.* I'm going to look fabulous today.

"You have five minutes before I knock again. After that, we're leaving without you."

I flip the door off and then groan as I roll out of the chair I'd been sitting in and get ready to face a predictably unpleasant day.

# 14
## REV

Caelynn's eyes are as red as I am sure mine are. Tyadin and I stayed up most of the night, reading through several books about the Schorchedlands and the Wicked Gates. We got very little new information.

Our strange party doesn't speak much at all as we set out, each with a mount this time. I ride my golden stag, and Tyadin provides plain old stocky ponies for himself and Caelynn, thanks to the Crumbling Counsel. He's a hero in this place ever since the trials. It's funny—he's a hero for placing in fifth. Drake, Kari, and Brielle, I know, each had to deal with legitimate backlash for simply not winning. Mostly for allowing a lesser court fae to defeat them.

Once we make it to the flat trail we set out on our trek at an easy gallop. As we grow closer, the sun finally rises enough to wake me fully and Tyadin as well, apparently, because he begins a chatter.

"So, you two traveled from the Luminescent Court together."

"Yes?" Caelynn says.

"With one mount? What happened to yours, Caelynn?"

"Never had one."

"You mean to say Prince Reveln of the Luminescent Court, *the gentleman*, made the lady walk the whole thirty-mile trek on foot while he rode that lovely stag?"

"I am not a lady," Caelynn spits quickly.

"You're a countess, are you not?" Ty asks.

"I was disinherited long ago. And we traveled much farther *on foot* during the trials. Thirty miles is not that far."

Even for fae, thirty miles isn't a particularly pleasant stroll, but I don't feel the need to add to Tyadin's tangent. I should just tell him to pipe down and mind his business now, but I'm curious to see Caelynn's reaction to this conversation.

"But we didn't have the option of a stag or a horse during the trials. It's really just about manners."

"I had plenty of manners. Of course, I offered her my stag."

"Ahh!" Tyadin says. "So, you walked then?"

"No."

There's a pause, and I notice Tyadin's lip twitch. Holding back a smile. "Don't tell me... You two shared a stag?" Tyadin asks, his eyebrows rising.

"Hush," Caelynn says, and we both ignore his snort.

The trees thin, the pathway becomes uneven and covered in weeds. There's very little reason for any fae to travel this direction. We all give the Schorchedlands a wide berth whenever possible. Who wants to travel near hell? No one. At least not anyone with good intentions. Of course, there are three times each year that the spirits inside can be beseeched. Living fae can make bargains with wraiths to do their bidding in exchange for temporary freedom from their hellish cage. But those kinds of deals aren't common.

Our party pauses, standing side by side at the edge of the forest. In front of us lies a plain of scraggly yellowed grass for a full mile before the huge wall of thorn shoots into the sky, shadowing everything around it for miles. No wonder the forest felt so bleak. The wall might be a lively bright green, but it's so imposing it pulls life from everything nearby until there is nothing left.

"All right, let's get this over with," I say, and I press my uncomfortable mount forward.

I hop off of Killian once he won't walk any closer to the thorn wall. This is our fourth trip here, you'd think he would be used to it by now. As useful as a mount like him would be, I'd never expect an animal to follow me through the walls because it would mean certain death.

Without looking back at my companions, I walk to the small opening beneath the red thorn arch. I step into the little cove. Thorns over my head send anxiety shooting through me, but I keep my chin high, determined.

I slit my forearm, wincing at the pain, and I press my hand over the red X. "I come to complete my mission." I tell the gates.

There's a long hiss as if a spirit within the wall is angry with me. Annoyed, is more likely, I suppose. How many times must it say no before I'll get the point?

*You may not pass.*

"Why!" I yell at it. "Just let me through!"

*You have completed your quest.*

I swallow. That's new. What does that mean?

Suddenly, my body is thrown from the vine cove and onto my butt in the middle of the field of deadened grass.

Tyadin holds out a hand to help me up. "Well that's rude," he says.

"It's annoyed with me."

"What did it say? The same message?" Caelynn asks.

"No. This time is said 'You may not pass. You've completed your quest.' Which obviously, I haven't."

Caelynn narrows her eyes and purses her lips. "Didn't I hear the scourge had stopped spreading?"

I nod. "It hasn't spread in two weeks."

"Maybe it knows you don't need to enter because the curse has already ended? Maybe it's finished, and everyone will just assume you did your job."

"Sure, until it hits again and I look like a fool."

She pulls in a long breath through her nose. Then, she taps her fingertips on her knee and begins to pace.

"I'm going to do a quick pass down the line of the wall," Tyadin says, and then guides his pony away from us.

"You really think it's over? Just like that? That easy?"

Caelynn laughs. "Life is never that easy, huh?"

"Never."

"We'll keep thinking, okay?"

"I know. I didn't actually expect the gate to just suddenly let me in. It's just frustrating. I feel... stupid. Like I have to be missing something so obvious." I shrug, trying to keep the bitterness from reaching my chest. I don't need to feel those things, not now. I don't need to let the tears fall. Not again. Not in front of her.

# 15

## REV

"So," Ty says, lying back on the red velvet couch, arm hitched behind his head. "You and Caelynn."

I raise my eyebrows but say nothing. We'd spent the last few hours reading through more books. Caelynn left an hour ago to go rest. She hadn't slept much over the last two days, so we essentially pushed her out. I wouldn't be surprised to find out instead of napping she's reading the same books over again in her room.

I take another bite of cucumber and cheese from the plate Tyadin had brought for us and ignore his prying question. We don't have many meals in this palace as it's more of a distraction than anything. We aren't the only guests causing a commotion, so we only head to the banquet hall when we require a full mental break from our endeavor.

"What's going on there?"

"Nothing. She's my ally. I needed help, so she's helping."

Tyadin chuckles. "She's your fated mate, Rev. There's

no such thing as just friends—or allies, whatever you want to call it—with your fucking soulmate."

I grind my teeth. "It's complicated, yes. But what am I supposed to do? She's a convicted criminal that's hated by everyone. We have no future together even if I could forgive her."

"Could?" Ty sits up, looking me right in the eye. "You're telling me you haven't already forgiven her?"

"She killed my brother, Ty," I say through gritted teeth.

"Why?" he asks calmly, his eyes never leaving mine. A challenge.

Is he serious right now? Anxiety crawls in my gut.

"There was a reason, wasn't there?" He crosses his arms. Damn nosy fae-dwarf...

I look down at my folded hands and don't respond.

"Fate doesn't make that big of a mistake, Rev. There's meaning behind all of it. I don't know her whole story, but I suspect you know more than I do. I can see it in the way you look at her. I can see it in the way you're comfortable around her. How you look to her for help and confirmation. How you only decided to trust me with this," he waves vaguely, "at her prompting."

My eyes flash to his, but he gives no sign he's upset. "How did you know about that?"

"Put two and two together. You wouldn't have come if not for her." He shrugs. "It's fine. You have a hard time trusting. This is hard for you."

I press my fists to my lips.

"My point is that you trusted her."

"So what?" I finally admit, the pit in my stomach growing.

"So, you wouldn't trust her like that, mate or not, if you still hated her for those actions a decade ago."

I swallow. "What does it matter? I don't hate her. I trust her more than I should. But there is no future for us. The magic of fated mates is not that powerful, Ty. Once I secure the cure, she'll be banished. And even if that wasn't true, do you think the Luminescent Court people could ever accept her as their queen?" I let out a bitter laugh.

"You're embarrassed of her? You don't want them to know?" Ty guesses, and I stand suddenly, the tension in my shoulders growing to the point of pain.

"There is no hope!" I say loudly. "So, why put that wedge between me and my people? Why put us through that pain? It's not worth it."

Tyadin leans forward, his hands are folded at his chin and pointer fingers over his lips as he looks thoughtfully at the table between us. He's quiet for a long while.

My heart pounds hard. Part of me wants to tell Tyadin off. Tell him to mind his own damn business. But I know he means well, and the truth is I don't want to lose another friend. So, I swallow down my anger and pain, and I close my eyes tightly.

"It would be worth it, if it was me," Ty says quietly, finally breaking the silence.

"You've got a crush on Cae?" I ask lightly, successfully breaking my own anxiety and his as well, apparently, because he chuckles. It fades quickly, though.

"I saw my mate in that orb too," he tells me, and I take my seat, leaning back and waiting for him to continue.

"And?" I prompt.

His eyes flash to mine. "I don't know her. Never seen

her. But now her face is in my mind all the time. When will I meet her? Will I ever get the chance? I spend a lot of time thinking about that."

I lay my head back on the couch, looking up at the stone ceiling.

"And when I see you with Caelynn... I sometimes put myself in your place. I can see how much it would hurt. How confusing it could be. But I know that even if my mate had done something terrible, I'd want her. Maybe I wouldn't give up everything for her—or maybe I would, I don't know. But I know I'd steal what moments I could. I'd want the chance to... at least know what it feels like."

I blink back tears and then clear my throat. "I have to live the rest of my life without her," I say slowly, eyes closed. "I'd rather not know what I'm missing."

"If it were me," Ty says slowly. "I'd rather die fighting for my dreams than live with regret and wonder *what if.*"

"Damn it, Ty."

"Does that not also count for broken hearts?"

I shake my head. "It's different."

"Yeah," he says, his tone making it clear he doesn't at all mean it. "It does make me wonder, though."

"What?"

"The books said the gate would only let people enter the Schorchedlands if they sincerely asked, with no coercion. What if... what if part of you doesn't want to go?"

The ache in my stomach grows, but I don't speak as his words sink in.

"Once you go inside, you lose your chance. You either die inside or you succeed. If you come back out with the cure, Caelynn leaves forever. The moment you enter those gates, you lose her."

I press my eyes closed.

"Maybe the gates can feel that. The hesitancy."

"I don't have any hesitancy," I say, my voice weak. I haven't ever, not once, thought those things. I haven't wished for a chance to be with her. I haven't feared the day she'd leave. So, I don't buy his theory but...

"Are you absolutely sure?" he prods. "When you make your request to the Wicked Gates, is your heart completely convinced it's what you want? Not just what you're told to do? Because that was clear, you can't be forced into it."

I nod. "Maybe that was the whole reason for the trials. To make sure the person chosen to be savior really wanted it. Maybe I failed in that part." I swallow.

I take in a long deep breath, and Ty just watches me expectantly.

"All right, it's worth a shot. Convince the gates I *want* to go in. I do. I want to be the savior. I want to prove my father wrong. I want to take my place in my court, maybe even the High Court, with or without my father's support."

"Maybe another trip to the thorn wall is in order?"

I'm not looking forward to it, but I steel my heart, preparing myself. No stray thoughts of the mate I'll never have. No more torturing myself with her closeness.

It's time for me to fulfill my destiny.

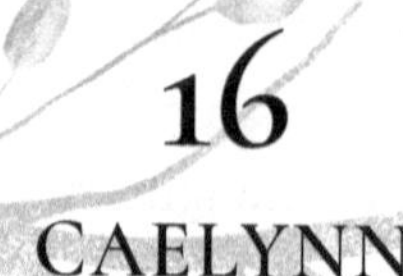

# 16

## CAELYNN

Two days full of a shit ton of reading, and I'm no closer to helping Rev get through the gates to hell. If only that were as good as it sounds.

But Rev and Ty seem to have come up with a theory. They wouldn't tell me what it was, but Rev left after a large breakfast to head for the wall—alone.

The dwarves and fae of this palace chatter behind me as I stare out the window of the banquet hall, absently examining at the mountains. There's an expansive view from this spot and I could almost pretend that deep in the distance, where the horizon grows darker in one small spot, it's the shadow lands. My home.

Somewhere beyond these mountain ranges is my homeland, that's true whether it's visible or not.

If Rev was to finally gain access to the Schorchedlands, I could go. I could finally complete my personal mission. Walkthrough the gates of the Shadow Court palace with my head high. I could touch the black fountain and fuel it with my magic.

I could kneel before the queen and receive my welcome into her court.

The one thing I've been seeking since I was a child. Such a simple quest I've failed at again and again.

But my heart still stupidly aches at the thought of Rev leaving. It's senseless, I know. But being around him makes me feel more complete than I have in a long time. It's sad to think of losing that feeling.

Even if it is was always inevitable. I'm just glad I had the moments I did. They were so much more than I could have ever hoped for.

"You all right?"

I jump and turn to face Tyadin.

"Don't sneak up on me like that," I say and smack him on the arm.

"Hey-hey, that's an act of war, young lady."

I snort. "Who are you going to fight? The Shadow Court? Or the human realm?"

He shrugs. "Just you."

I tap him on the cheek in a mock smack and wink. "As I've said many times, you'll have to get in line. I have many enemies."

"You know I'll stand with you," he says, his expression growing serious, "if you ever need it."

I swallow. It's the nicest offer anyone has ever made. "Thanks," I say honestly. "I'm my own worst enemy most days."

He smiles. "I'll stand with you then too."

I smile, holding back tears. *No need to be a wuss, Cae.* "Seems like you've got your hands full with just Rev."

"Well, isn't that true? With any luck, he'll have it under control after today."

"Right," I say quietly. I look behind him, where a group of young fae females whisper, eyes darting my direction. For the most part, the few dozen fae living in this palace have gotten used to mine and Rev's presence, but I do still have a fan or two—or three, in this case—that hang around, watching me. Those girls had me sign an image of a shadow-vyrn yesterday evening. Apparently, that wasn't enough for them, though.

It's a strange feeling to be admired.

Admired for something I'm able to be proud of, at least.

Everyone else has their attention on a bulky male sitting at a table with two other dwarves. He's huge, in width, not height. His beard is thick but trimmed. His eyes a piercing deep blue and his cheekbones as sharp as any fae. He's handsome, in a rugged kind of way.

The potential dwarf king stares at his plate, barely touching his food, his face hard as stone, gaze hyper-focused, like the answers to the universe could be found in his chicken broth.

"He's got the brooding hero thing down," I say, shamelessly changing the subject. It's an easy one with Tyadin, though. His eyes light up just with the mention of his new hero.

"He's a bit serious," Tyadin says. "But from what I've heard, he hasn't had a very pleasant life."

"I suppose that's true."

"Apparently, he remembers it. All of it. The shadow creature that destroyed the throne and his father. The wars over him and his brother. The goblins. And he's been on the run since then. No one would take him in, thinking he'd inspire a dwarfish rebellion, and sweep their dwarfish servants away."

"Why would they care? Aren't dwarfs second-class citizens in most courts?"

Tyadin nods. "But we're very useful. In many places, we're treated like slaves. We do the stonework to make their castles beautiful without requiring magic to keep them standing, but we're paid very little and then not welcomed by the other fae. If all the dwarfs were to leave, the fae would have to rebuild their own structures. Some of them can but never with the same quality or ease. No one can mine or carve stone the way dwarves can."

"Well, that sucks for your king guy," I say awkwardly. "What's his name?"

"Torrick Strongbane."

"When does this quest of yours begin?"

Tyadin shrugs. "Hopefully soon, but there's no real telling. Torrick is gathering support—albeit with little success. Once he decides there's nowhere else to turn, he'll set off. And I'll follow."

"Whenever that happens to be, Ty, I wish you all the best. And if I ever have the chance to make my way to my own kingdom, I'll make sure the queen is ready to aid your party if ever needed." I smile sincerely.

"I'm glad I became your accidental ally during the game," Ty says.

"I'm glad I was finally able to wear you down." I wink.

"Oh, whatever. You needed me."

"I did indeed."

It's near sunset when I spy a mount and rider crossing the narrow bridge in the distance, its silhouette flying at top speed.

It's impossible to tell if the animal is horse or stag, but the likelihood of it being someone else seems low.

I'd spent a good portion of the day standing watch in case Rev came riding in. If I saw him over the winding mountains, it would mean his mission today failed. I shouldn't want that.

When I do finally see a form that's very likely him, part of me is terrified. Part of me is relieved. I never did claim to be a good person.

I rush down to the canal entrances, and by the time I reach the dark tunnels, a series of crashes are echoing off the walls. I sprint the rest of the way until I reach the open entryway—massive oak doors to the front of the castle. The shadows shift in the orange glow of the scattered torchlight. I stop as I see a broad-shouldered fae slam a candle into the floor with a clatter. My breath catches, heart hammering in my chest.

Rev is here. He's safe. But the rage on his face tells me he's anything but okay.

He grabs an already splintered frame and smashes it onto the ground, groaning with each breath like he's trying not to sob. He desperately kicks at the pieces of splintered wood still daring to cling together.

"Rev," I say, but my voice is still almost lost in the bombardment of clatters. More items join the others on the floor, a book, a shattered vase—the flowers it once housed flutters to the ground gracefully.

I rush forward and grab the golden statue of a dwarf from his hands. He tries to rip it away from me, an angry snarl on his lips. His eyes are nearly totally black.

"Stop it," I demand. His black eyes find mine. He's found a new target, I realize with a jolt just a moment before he slams me to the wall. His shaking hand is around my throat, his nose inches from mine.

I wince but don't fight back. "Rev," I breathe. At least he's stopped tearing apart an allied court's castle décor. His grip lessens as his shaking increases, a small bit of color returns to his eyes. His rage twists into pain, and it's like a stab to my gut.

I'm desperate to know what happened today. What took him so long? On his stag, a trip to the wall and back would only take about two hours' time. He was gone for twelve. What happened in between?

"Are you hurt?" I ask, my voice is soft but strained.

He blinks, meeting my eye with recognition for the first time. His eyes are bloodshot, but the grey returns. He drops his hand away from my throat and steps away.

I swallow.

"What would have hurt me? There isn't anything to fight!" he yells, hands tossed into the air. "There's no one standing in my way. No one to kill, nothing to maim. Nothing I can DO!" He swipes at another table, Crumbling Court décor crashing to the floor and shattering. I wince.

He turns again and presses his forehead to the stone wall as sobs wrack his body. *Shit,* I think. Tears well in my eyes as I feel a touch of the same helplessness he does. What am I supposed to do? How do I fix this?

I don't think I can.

A set of footsteps stomps from the hall behind me and a soldier appears, dumbstruck as he stares at the destruction.

"Can you go get Tyadin, please?" I ask the guard.

His eyes dart over the foyer and back to me. Then, he nods and rushes down the hall away from us. Hopefully, Tyadin can help clean this up without a massive diplomatic issue on our hands.

Rev screams in frustrated agony and punches at the stone wall. His fist collides with a sickening crack and blood splatters onto my shirt.

I jump forward and catch his wrist mid-swing and twist it before he's able to get a second hit in. It's my turn now to shove him against the wall, turning him to face me. One hand holds his blood-soaked wrist, and the other is pressed firmly on his chest.

"Stop it," I demand again. "I know you're hurting but you have to stop." My voice breaks, bottom lip trembling. I'm strong enough to stop him from hurting himself, but God does it hurt to see him like this.

And now I hate myself for hoping he'd return today. How selfish was that?

I know how important this mission is, but I'd stupidly feared losing him.

Rev's chest heaves beneath my hand; his broken eyes latch onto mine.

"Rev, what happened?" I ask in a whisper. His face

crumples, just like that. His shoulders slump, and he presses his face into my neck.

I suppress a shiver at the pleasure his breath sends cascading down my skin but well... *it's not the most ideal circumstances to get all hot and bothered, Cae.*

His chest shudders in a wave of sobs, and he collapses into my arms. Together, we sink to the ground in a heap of awkward limbs and tears.

I don't say anything more. There's nothing to say.

I know this moment. I've been there—more than once. It's rock bottom. The moment everything seems to collapse in on you. When even the light of stars hide behind the storm clouds, and there seems to be no hope left to grasp.

Rev is broken. Right here and now, he's at his most vulnerable. And there isn't anything to fix, I realize. So, I don't shush him or tell him it'll be okay. I just hold him and let him cry.

The fae prince of the Luminescent Court dissolves into tears in my arms.

Minutes later Tyadin arrives. At the sound of footsteps approaching, Rev clenches me closer, his face pressed tightly into my neck. Tyadin stops, his eyes wide as he surveys the foyer.

"What the hell happened?" he whispers. His lips part as he examines the broke Rev in my lap.

"I'm sorry," I say with an awkward grimace. But what else is there to say?

He swallows and lifts his head high, chest puffed out. "Can you get him out of here?"

I nod. "I'll get him to bed."

"I'll take care of the rest," Tyadin says with a determined set of his sharp jaw.

I prompt Rev to stand, and he obeys without much effort. I wrap his arm over my neck and grip him around the waist. His head hangs low—in exhaustion or shame, I'm not sure. I don't suppose it matters much. His feet only shuffle on the stone floor, but he follows my guidance down the hall and up the stairs to our rooms.

He pushes his bedroom door open but then pauses, resisting my pull for the first time.

"What's wrong?"

"Nothing," he whispers, and with a determined expression, he presses through the doorway, pulling me with him. I stumble forward, his arm still over my shoulders.

He marches to the bed, pulling me along with him until the moment he drops onto the mattress, face first.

He finds his way beneath the covers and groans, pressing his face into the pillow. I back away slowly, but he lifts himself up.

Is it entirely insane and wrong that I take his moment to admire the muscles on his back flex?

"Caelynn?" he says through a gruff voice.

"Yeah?" I whisper. Does he need something? Water? A potion?

"Will you stay with me?" he says weakly like it pains him to ask. My stomach sinks and heart lifts all at once.

It pains him to need me. To want me.

I swallow and pretend that fact doesn't hurt. But I couldn't possibly blame him.

"Of course," I say, even though my heart aches terribly as I eye the place beneath the sheets he carves out for me.

My breath trembles. Am I really going to do this to myself?

"I'll never leave you, so long as you want me."

It's not like I don't torture myself in every other way. Why not this too?

So, I crawl into the bed with Rev.

His arm slips beneath my head, and the other curls over my waist, pulling me closer. My breaths come shallow here, cocooned in Rev's chest and arms.

Tears sting my eyes, but I allow myself to fall into this feeling. His warmth fills everything, and in only moments, everything falls away. Every doubt, all the fear and pain, until all that's left is him.

Reveln. Mine.

I shake my head, a quick reminder not to fall. Not totally. Reveln is my mate, but he will never be mine. Not really.

# 17
## REV

My whole body is stiff and aching as I wake. The sun is only just peeking in through the window, and something beside me shifts.

I blink rapidly and pull away as I realize Caelynn is in my bed.

Holy shit.

I playback the events from last night and run my fingers through my hair. God, I'm an idiot. I seriously lost my shit. And she was there, holding me up. Holding me together.

Caelynn lies beside me, face as serene as I've ever seen her, her chest falling and rising in a calm rhythm. I watch her for a moment. Then, I pull a strand of blond hair from over her angelic face and tuck it behind her ear gently. I allow myself that one moment of delusion.

I let myself feel that desperate hope for what should have been but will never be.

Then, I sit back against the headboard and rub my face rigorously. *Back to reality, Rev.*

*Fuck.* Reality sucks. What the hell do I do now? I tried to enter the Schorchedlands and failed—again.

I'm a failure. An absolute complete failure. Everything my father ever said about me was right.

I tried to convince the gates to let me through three times yesterday. And when it continued to refuse me, I lost it there, I scratched at the bright green vines. I tried to climb the outside of the wall, resulting in cuts and scrapes all over my body.

The wall wouldn't let me in.

*You don't belong.*

I don't belong anywhere. I'm not a real prince, so that throne doesn't belong to me. My mate is a banished criminal who killed my brother. And now, the one quest I've been given doesn't want me either.

I'm as lost as I've ever been.

Caelynn stirs quietly, her body twisting and squirming as she wakes. Her eyes find mine and she smiles. "Morning," she says, with a surprised blink.

I let out a bitter snort but find amusement in watching her realize where she is. I take a deep breath and let it out slowly, staring up at the stone ceiling.

"Breakfast?" she asks without meeting my eye, and I can't help but smile. She's not going to comment on last night at all, is she? Why does it make me care for her even more? I press my eyes closed for one moment and then open them and allow a smile.

I climb out of bed but notice out of the corner of my eye how Caelynn's eyes linger on my chest. I resist the urge to point it out.

Nope. Our desire for one another is predictably intense,

but it's just the magic inside us trying to pull us together. Well, it's mostly the magic.

"Breakfast," I say, reminding myself what I'm supposed to be contemplating. "Yes. But not in the hall. Not today."

Caelynn sits up and stretches, her shirt rides up enough to expose a sliver of skin. I avert my eyes quickly.

"The sitting room, then?" she says. "We can get a tray delivered instead. I assume you're hungry."

I sigh. "Starving."

———

Tyadin is already in our meeting room when we arrive. He looks up and smiles, but then his eyes narrow like he's noticed something suspicious. I take a seat at the couch, shoulders slumped awkwardly. I have plenty to be bashful about that has nothing to do with the sexy shadow fae who happened to share my bed last night.

It didn't mean anything, but Ty wouldn't take it that way.

"Everything okay?" he asks. I nod slowly but don't meet his eye.

"Well enough," Caelynn answers. "How about you? Anything we need to do to assist the cleanup?"

*Oh, right.* I totally trashed a room in a court that is not my own. "I can pay for anything I—"

Tyadin waves me off. "It's fine. All taken care of."

I'm not entirely convinced, but I'll take the opportunity to let it go for now. I'll make sure I more than make up for whatever I destroyed. Assuming there wasn't anything priceless in that part of the castle. I hope I didn't destroy any Crumbling Court's heirlooms.

"Something came for you," Tyadin says casually to Caelynn, but the tense set of his jaw sends a jolt of anxiety through me.

I sit on the couch across from him, and he hands Caelynn a letter with the High Court's seal on it. My breath catches in my throat.

Caelynn got one too? My eyes are pinned to the envelope between her fingers. She stares at it like she's unsure if it something precious or if it will explode if she makes any sudden movements.

"Cae and I each got one," Ty says. "But nothing for you," he adds slowly.

I bite my lip and nod. "That's because I already got mine." I rummage in my pocket, push the gemstone farther down, and pull out a wrinkled parchment.

The invitation came via raven at the Wicked Gates yesterday. The bird circled overhead and then finally dropped the envelope right onto my stag's saddle after my second failed attempt at getting through.

It's like it was watching to see if I'd fail first before delivering a message from the queen. Stupid bird. The queen's message may have played a role in my breakdown yesterday.

My stomach aches, thinking about what might be inside the letters. The queen obviously knows where I am, and if Caelynn is also receiving mail here, she must be keeping tabs on her too.

I don't like that thought one bit.

Is she choosing Caelynn as her new savior? Is she planning to declare me an official failure?

I unfold the crumpled and ripped parchment.

My fingers run over the calligraphy writing on elaborately-decorated parchment.

**Prince Reveln,**

**The High Queen Zanter-Leisha has requested your presence at the Royal Gala this weekend.**

Beneath the formal letter with a date and time is a more casual scrawl from the queen herself.

***Unless you are inside the Schorchedlands at the time of the event, I expect you to attend.***

I drop the invitation on the table in front of me, staring wide-eyed. Waiting for my allies' reaction. Do they see what I see? A veiled threat.

They don't speak for several long moments.

"Why would she even want me there?" I say, tossing my hands up. "She doesn't, does she? She's telling me I better be in the Schorchedlands by then."

Because the other option is that, in days, I'll be expected to parade in front of hundreds of fae at the High Court and pretend I'm not an utter failure.

I eye a similar invitation in Caelynn's grip. Tyadin's is the same.

Each of us were invited to a last-minute High Court ball.

"Is it a test? Is she giving up on me as champion? If I show up at the ball, she's going to announce Caelynn as the new champion."

Why else invite Caelynn as well? She's not well-liked by anyone of merit in the High Court; in fact, many wish her dead. But she *is* the runner up of the trials.

"No." Caelynn smiles, but it doesn't reach her eyes. "She wants to put on a confident face," she says smoothly, her eyes holding mine for longer than usual. She's studying me. She's concerned for me.

I don't blame her. I am too.

If the people of the realm, any of them, learn that I can't get inside the Schorchedlands...

"The scourge has stopped spreading, so the people will be at ease, and seeing you could make them feel even better," Tyadin muses.

"Lulls in the spread have happened before," I tell them. "And they're historically followed by a huge attack. More children will die before it's over. Showing up to this gala is a terrible idea." I press my palms to my eyes.

"You'll just have to trust her." Her smile is forced.

I shake my head, stomach sinking. Over and over, I've failed. "She wants me to fail," I say, voice dead.

Caelynn's hand drops to my forearm, and I blink at her delicate fingers touching me. "Then, she's in for one hell of a fight. I won't rest until you win this."

I clench my jaw. "Me or we?" The words slip out before I even consider them.

Her eyebrows pull down. "What?"

*What if Caelynn is hoping I fail, so she can take my place as savior?*

My breaths come out quick and shallow. I look up and meet her darkened stare, concern so damn clear it's insane I'd consider anything different.

Well, if it's not true, it should be. "Maybe you should go," I say. She may not be *hoping* for the chance to fix her mistake in the trials, but maybe she's the right one for the job.

"No." Her voice is sharp. She pulls her hand away and crosses her arms, her jaw set.

"At least if you try," I say calmly as hopelessness seeps into my bones, "we'll know if some of our theories hold merit."

"And if they do, I'll be the one in the Schorchedlands. It can't be undone."

I bite my lip. "Then, you'll be the hero and so be it."

"No," she says again. "I will not take this from you unless it's a last resort. I know what it will mean for you if someone else completes the quest."

"And what does it mean for you?" I spit. "There's no happy ending for both of us, Cae. I was prepared to take this reward without even considering how selfish it is..."

Without considering what it could mean for Caelynn if she were to earn back her place in our realm.

"Stop," she says, angry eyes pinned to mine. "My life is what it is because of my own deeds. I deserve the punishment. You do not."

Caelynn drops to her knees before me and places a hand on my thigh. She looks up at me with fierce eyes. "Look at me," she demands. She grips my chin beneath harsh fingers when I don't obey, and she forces my gaze up to hers. "You deserve this," she tells me. "What we did, we did together. You saved my heart. I wouldn't have ever gotten over Raven's death. Never. It would have destroyed me in ways Brielle and Drake never would have been able to comprehend. You deserved the win as much as me, if not more."

I narrow my eyes, watching her.

"You are worthy of this, Rev. And I will not let you give up."

I swallow.

"Me neither." Tyadin steps forward, getting down on one knee before me. "I believe in you, Prince Reveln. My future king."

I let out a huff that's part laugh, part cry. "At least until your dwarf kings takes back his kingdom."

Tyadin's eyes shine. "A man can have two kings."

"We can figure this out," Caelynn says. "Do not let the queen or your father or anyone else see your weakness."

"They'll exploit it," Ty agrees.

"So, you're going to show up to that gala, with your head high and eyes bright. And you'll show them the kind of leader you will be. Brave and poised, even in the face of adversity."

I cover my mouth in my hand, not even believing what I'm hearing. From her. Caelynn of the Shadow Court. My brother's murderer. The fae I vowed to kill.

And right now, she's the only thing holding me together.

# 18
## CAELYNN

I sprawl out on the luxurious bed in my own room and stare at the invitation. The High Queen invited me, Caelynn of the Shadow Court, to a ball. Average members of the Shadow Court haven't been invited to events like this in several hundred years. The Shadow Court queen hasn't even been invited to ruling court events in a decade.

The fact that I was invited is significant, even if Rev doesn't understand how much. I don't know if the queen has ulterior motives, but I can't discount the message this sends.

The Shadow Court matters.

There's a gentle knock on my door, so I leave my invitation on my pillow and hop up to answer it. Tyadin leans against the frame, his hands in his pockets.

"What's up?" I ask.

"Just checking on you," he says.

I hold the door open wide, inviting him in. He enters

slowly, eyeing the parchment on my pillow. "It's crazy, isn't it?" he says. "Being invited to the High Court palace."

I rock back on my heels. "Yeah."

"No one from the Crumbling Court has ever been invited."

"Ever?"

He shakes his head. "One of the reasons the trials were such a big deal for us. They'd never recognized us as a court before."

"That's crazy." The Crumbling Court was once part of the Crystal Court, but civil war involving the dwarves caused a split about eighty years ago. "How do you feel about it? The gala?"

He walks to the window on the far side of the room and leans against the wall beside it. "Bittersweet, I guess. You?"

I nod. "Yeah. It's strange. But also... kind of amazing. Even if it won't change things for me personally, it gives me hope for my court. And maybe it will give my people hope. They need it."

He smiles. "I doubt many dwarves have been invited either."

"True." I hadn't even considered that.

"I'd never owned any formal wear until the trials. I don't know much about dresses, but we have a dressmaker I can send up for you."

I smile and nod, accepting his offer. I'm capable of creating something entirely out of magic, but there are downsides to that tactic. Something made of magic can be unraveled by magic. That's not usually much of a risk in high society, but as notoriously hated as I am... well, I wouldn't put it past someone to recognize the magic binding the fabric and playing a joke on me. Not worth it.

"That would be wonderful, thank you."

"How is Rev?" he asks. "I'm concerned about him."

I bite my lip. "Yeah, he's... I don't know. He hasn't broken down again, not like before. But it's weighing on him. He needs us."

"He needs you," Ty says. "You're holding him together right now."

I open my mouth to respond but shut it, deciding it'd be better not to say anything at all. I care for Rev, but I won't dare let myself hope. I won't let myself fall for a fae prince I can never have.

I'll give up anything to save him—anything except my heart. That, I'll keep locked away forever.

# 19
## REV

I wring my hands anxiously as I wait in the foyer. There are fewer items decorating the tables here, and that simple realization has my stomach sinking. The fae portrait is back in its place on the wall, but it's missing its frame. No one has said a word about the damage I caused. Maybe Ty came up with some excuse that didn't involve me. I don't even know.

I try to convince myself that I don't care, but deep down it eats away at me.

Guilt for my own weakness. A king wouldn't act that way. Maybe my father is right and I'm not worthy of the crown. Any crown.

I shake my head. Confidence. Ty and Cae are right, faking my way through tonight is my only course of action. I need to prove to the queen I am still the right choice for savior. I can do this.

Even if doubts are now eating away at me, I can't let her know that. *Don't let them see your weakness.*

The clinking of heels alerts me to someone approaching, and my stomach does summersaults as Caelynn nears. Her hair is pulled back and decorated with tiny glowing gemstones that look like pixies.

Her dress is a simple sea green, low cut, and cinched at the waist, hugging her gentle curves. There are several strands of curls that fall down her bare back. She wears a string of lovely gemstones around her neck.

My mind jumps to the Lumistone still in my pocket.

Tyadin walks beside her, wearing an ensemble of war-ready armor. Leathers and golden chest plate. All he's missing is a helmet and battle-ax.

I raise my eyebrows as he approaches. "Who are we fighting tonight, friend?"

Ty smiles. "Anyone we want."

"Preferably no one," Caelynn adds seriously. I smirk at her and red crosses her cheeks. I pretend not to notice.

"You look good," I tell them both. Tyadin's attire is less traditional but still formal in appearance. I quite like it actually. He'll stand out but in a good way.

Tyadin nods, and that's all the small talk my odd crew has in them tonight. We walk together down the dark hall and find a carriage waiting for us. The last gift the Crumbling Court offered was the use of a mahogany carriage adorned with lovely yellow gemstones. It's very clear which court it belongs to, which is exactly the point.

The Crumbling Court wants to show off that they're hosting the Luminescent Court prince, Trial of Thorn's victor, and potential High Heir. I don't mind. I'm used to the politics. And a little added reputation is the least I can do after my behavior the other night.

Once we head inside the carriage, the world around us

disappears, and for just a little while, it's only me, Ty, and Caelynn. The two people I trust most in the world. As odd as that is.

As soon as the carriage begins making its way, Tyadin grins and pulls out a bottle. "To help us loosen up a bit," he says, wiggling his eyebrows.

"You're so lame," Caelynn says, but her lips curl into an amused smile.

He pops the lid of the fire whiskey and takes a swig before handing it to Cae. "Wait!" she says. "We're not going over that narrow stone bridge in this thing, are we?"

Ty laughs. "No, we're taking a different route. You two took the back-way in."

"Good," she says, and her shoulders relax. I chuckle.

"What?" she spits, her eyes shining with that lovely gold I've come to adore.

"Oh, nothing." I grab the bottle and take a long swig.

Our journey to the High Court will be significantly longer than I'm used to. The Luminescent Court has a portal directly there—all of the ruling courts do. They're highly guarded and blocked until invited by the queen, but they make it convenient for travel to and from the High Court. A few minutes ride, and we're there.

The Crumbling Court doesn't have any portals at all, unfortunately. We had considered traveling the thirty miles to the Schorchedlands portal then to the Luminescent Court and through their portal. We decided instead to request passage through the Crystal Court's portal. It's essentially the same distance, but it allows us to avoid my father.

The Crystal Court was easy to contact. I sent a quick

note to Kari via falcon. She set it all up in a matter of minutes, and I heard back within the hour that our passage was set.

So, now, we'll need to spend an hour in the carriage before reaching the portal, but with good company and fire whiskey, I find myself glad to have this time away from prying eyes and expectations. It'll be short-lived, but the laughter we share is just the tonic I need.

———

Half the bottle of fire whiskey is gone before the Crystal Court is in sight. The castle is tall, nearly the whole thing made of purple crystal, shooting haphazardly into the sky. If I didn't know better, I'd think it was a strange mountain, as opposed to a castle. As we get closer, though, we can see more details that give it away. Windows and balconies and flags flying on the topmost towers.

"Wow," Caelynn breathes.

"Never seen it?" Ty asks.

She shakes her head. "I can count the courts I've been to on one hand. This was not one."

"I've only seen it from a distance," Ty says. "There's a mountain pass just to the north of the palace that's common enough for dwarfish travels and had a good vantage. I've never been through its gates, though. I didn't think I ever would. But then again, I never thought I'd be living inside the Crumbling Court palace either."

"Life is never quite what we expect," Caelynn says, staring out the window as we glide smoothly down the mountain pass. "Good or bad. It's never what we expect."

I sit back in the seat and lay my head back. My mind already spinning. We're getting close now. Soon, those prying eyes will stick to me. They'll ask questions.

Questions I can't answer. How am I supposed to answer them?

"You all right?" Ty asks, patting me on the back.

I breathe in through my nose and out through my mouth. "What am I supposed to say? When people ask me about the cure, about the Schorchedlands?"

Caelynn drops the window curtain, her entire attention back on me. "Change the subject. Brush them off. It's none of their business."

I press my palms to my eyes. "It's fine," I say, more to myself than them.

"Make a joke," Tyadin suggests. "We can come up with something witty. 'Schorchedlands were great, I met your mom there'."

Caelynn laughs but grimaces and smacks Ty on the back of the head. "Mom jokes, that's what you're resorting to?"

He shrugs but already the pressure on my chest has lessened.

"Just pull the dark and brooding thing. That's what I do," she says.

"You do have that role perfected. Got any tips?"

She shrugs but then considers seriously. "Keep your face flat, no emotion. Helps if you focus on the things that make you angry. Look off into the distance when people talk to you. No smiles. No jokes. Keep moving through the crowd like you have somewhere to be."

"It's better than mom jokes."

Caelynn snorts, and Ty hollers. "Hey! I coulda come up with something better, I was just warming up."

We laugh and take another round of shots; my blood warms and heart is comforted. My stomach still squirms uncomfortably, but I take long looks at my friends and know this is a moment I'll keep with me forever, no matter what else happens.

# 20

## CAELYNN

The carriage glides so much smoother than I'd have ever expected. I assume magic steadies the wheels and cabin because even a car couldn't ride this smooth on this sort of rough terrain in the human world. We pull back the curtains and watch as we pass through the crystal gates and onto palace grounds. The massive crystal towers looms over us. The colors vary, deep purple at the base into an amber in the middle and then a light lavender at the topmost tower.

I can't believe this place is real.

"Did dwarves build this palace?" I ask.

"Not the outside. A lot of the palace itself is natural, just enhanced, and carved out to become inhabitable. But you'd find many dwarf-mined gems decorating the inside and even the grounds. The sugilite pathways and banisters were dwarf made. Even so, the palace is very impressive."

I nod, it is.

There are three crystal-covered carriages waiting outside the front steps to the massive structure, and we pass by them toward an elaborate archway. The portal, I realize. My heart pounds harder as we approach. In moments we'll be on the High Court island. Where my ancestors once ruled.

A cool mist settles over my skin the moment we pass through the archway, and I blink as the magic stirs in the air. The sun has long since set here, the sky scattered with stars.

Rev stares straight ahead, jaw clenched and eyes unfocused. I give his hand a gentle squeeze, and he flinches, eyes darting to mine in surprise.

"You got this," I tell him.

His lips part, but then the carriage comes to a jerking stop and whispering begins as the fae outside realize who's inside the Crumbling Court carriage.

*"Is it Rev?"*

*"Rev is here?"*

*"He's with the dwarf court? That's weird, isn't it?"*

*"They're helping him defeat the scourge,"* someone says proudly, and Tyadin's eyes shine. His court's reputation has risen significantly in recent months. Even though he'll be leaving it all behind soon, I know it means a lot to him.

"You go first," I tell Ty. Let him have his moment. While the attention is on us completely.

"You two will walk in together?" Ty asks. "I'll walk in alone, I don't mind."

My eyes grow wide. I hadn't considered...

"No," Rev says quickly, and my stomach drops. I hadn't expected us to walk in as a couple or anything, but his tone has my heart aching. "I—" he stutters. "I'll go in alone."

His eyes meet mine, one part hard and determined, one part pitying.

*Perfect.* I repress an eye roll and smile. "Of course," I say sweetly, eyes cast to the ground.

Ty narrows his eyes and frowns disapprovingly at Rev. But then, he opens the door and hops out of the carriage in one smooth motion.

I watch as he marches through the gathering crowd proudly.

Soft fingertips glide over my ear, tucking a strand of hair behind it. "I'm sorry..." he says. "I just... I don't want to give them the wrong idea."

My blood runs cold, heart beating faster. *The wrong idea.*

God, it's stupid for that to hurt as much as it does. I know there's nothing between us. I know there's no hope of a future for us. We're not together, and we never will be.

But damn if it doesn't sting to know that my own fated mate is embarrassed of me.

That's what his real issue is. No one knows we're mates, so us walking in together wouldn't imply anything more than allies or at most a fling. In fact, it would deflect some of the attention he's so nervous about.

Walk in with me, keep their whispers focused on *us,* and they'll pay much less attention to the fact that he's not in the Schorchedlands. But he doesn't want that. Because he doesn't want to be seen with me any more than he already is.

Several moments pass in silence. Rev finally gives up and exits the carriage on his own. I close my eyes and let out a shuddering breath, pain washing over me.

*It's okay.* This is what I'm good at.

I'll never be what Rev needs. I'll never be the girl I was supposed to be.

Sometimes, I think I see it. The way he looks at me. The adoration I've so longed for. But then, he remembers. He sees the monster inside. He could have loved me, if things were different. He would have. The more time I spend with him, the more that truth is solidified.

We would have been perfect together, if not for the Night Bringer. My nightmare. He carved my soul right out of my body but left me living. Just enough to know the pain of the loss. To recognize what could have been.

I curl my darkness around me, anger and pain and rage and defeat. Dark ripples cast over me like wings, simmering like smoke falling off my body.

I'd almost forgotten who I am, hiding away with Rev and Tyadin where I could be just Cae, innocent and free. But no, that's not who I really am.

I am the villain.

To these fae here, and even Rev, I am a shadow fae murderer.

So, like so many times before, I'll play the part again. I'll use my pain as my strength and be who they all expect.

My expression falls into that cold indifferent mask I've worn so many times, and I march into the crowd of murmuring fae that parts for me as if I were the plague itself.

A yellow-eyed fae with glimmering gold horns gasps as I march past her, head high, eyes distant. "It's the murderer," she says.

*"What is she doing here?"*

*"Did she come with Rev?"*

Rev watches me, eyes darkened, but I avoid his gaze. With so much attention, it's a challenge to get away and find a shadowed corner where I can disappear entirely, but behind a large, twisted green tree, I find my opening. I duck behind the tree and curl my shadows around me until I'm all but invisible to the fae around me.

This is where I belong. Hiding in the shadows. My only real friends.

# 21
## REV

*S*hit.

That's the extent of my very eloquent thought process as Caelynn marches into the crowd with her head high, face slack and eyes hooded. Once, I would have believed her act.

Powerful. Indifferent. Intimidating.

She marches through the whispering crowd that hates her. It's the exact reason I didn't want to be seen with her, but, God, my gut twists as I watch her face them alone.

I should have been there. I should have stood beside her, damn the consequences. Because now, I know better, and I can see the pain through her façade.

She disappears into the crowd without looking in my direction, and I know I've failed her.

# 22

## CAELYNN

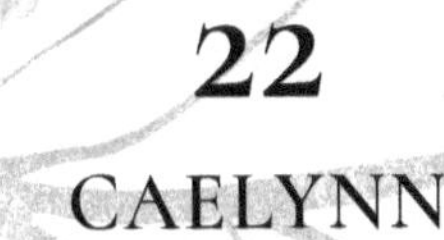

I watch from the corner shadows inside the grand hall as Prince Reveln of the Luminescent Court is presented to the High Court and marches down the largest set of stairs I've ever seen.

The room is full, the lights dimmed, making it very easy for me to slip to and from without a glance in my direction. It was easy to sneak my way into the grand hall without being "introduced."

Rev walks down the stairway, hand gliding over the banister made of intricate golden vines with actual living flowers. They look like metalwork, but they're real living plants. A gift from the previous Twisted Court King.

His eyes are hardened and distant, his shoulders back and head high. In this moment, I first picture him as the king he could be. Should be. Here in the High Court, the most powerful kingdom in the most powerful realm in the universe.

He fits the part. Perfectly.

Rev reaches the main floor, his first step echoing

through the hall, but the step after is lost in the encouraging murmurs. The floor is translucent glass, thick and glistening but clearly showcasing the tossing waves that crash a hundred feet beneath the hall.

The High Court is on an island of its own on the west side of the realm, and the palace here is the most intricate and incredible thing I've ever seen. It's a combination of every past ruling court's element. The walls are decorated with living vines, flickering in blue flame and flowers with sparkling centers. There is a massive chandelier over the steps that drips with incredible, eternal ice crystals.

Every court that has ruled here has left its mark.

Once Rev slips into the crowd with roaring applause, I turn my attention to the second most beautiful sight in the room.

The ceiling is a deep black void, unending, covered in gobs and gobs of glittering stars. Like its own expanding galaxy.

*Without the dark, there would be no light.* My mother used to say that. It's a bittersweet thought. Because I know I own all of the darkness. My darkness and pain will allow him to have light in his life.

I'm willing to make that sacrifice.

The ceiling, I recall from my childhood history books, was a gift from the Shadow Court. It's been here for over a thousand years, unchanged. I'd half expected it to be replaced with something new. The Shadow Court is no longer allowed to rule this place. Why keep its signature on it?

Because no one could do it better, I decide. The star-scattered ceiling is incredible.

"What the hell are you doing here?" a deep female voice calls over the crowd, and my stomach sinks. I spin to see a lovely purple-eyed, dark-skinned female marching toward me.

Kari's voice sounded harsh, but even though I'd almost killed her during the trials, I thought we ended on good terms. I could have killed her or even just left her to die, but instead, I gave her enough aid to save her life.

She stomps toward me, and then her arms are around me before I blink again. *What the hell?*

I drop my shadows because, clearly, they didn't work on her.

She releases me and smiles. "I thought you were back in the human world looking after your raven friend."

I blink. Kari was the Crystal Court champion in the trials, and she had a front-row seat for Raven's death and resurrection.

"I was. But... well, it's a long story. I have some unfinished business here and only so much time before my banishment is reinstated for good."

She nods slowly. "Are you here with Rev?"

My eyebrows pull down. "Why would I be here with Rev?"

"Oh," she says sheepishly, "it's just that I... well, it seems unlikely you'd have been invited."

I let out a bitter laugh. "Well, I was."

"Oh!" she says, eyes widening. "I'm sorry—"

I waive it off. "It's fine; I'd have assumed the same thing. I was shocked to get an invitation. I'm still expecting an ambush at any moment."

She giggles, but I'm entirely serious. A large number of people here want me dead.

A long-haired, arrogant fae with amber eyes enters the hall and marches down the stairs dramatically. Another person I'd rather not meet face to face. Not that Drake would show his animosity in the slightest. He's charming and cares about his reputation far too much.

He'd surely find a way to make me squirm, though.

"Let's get a drink," I declare, hoping she too would like to avoid her old ally.

"That's a fantastic idea." Kari leads me across the room, and I dart through the crowd, twisting through the shadows, hoping to keep unnoticed by most.

"You don't have to hide. No one will say or do anything to you tonight," she tells me.

"Their eyes will say plenty, even if their tongues don't."

"You don't strike me as the kind of fae who cares how people *look* at you." Kari grabs a tall glass of sparkling liquid and a short glass with purple liquid from a waiter's tray. She hands me both.

"What is this?"

"Crystal Court delicacy. Humans call it a Jager bomb."

I bust out laughing. "What?"

She chuckles alongside me. "It's a joke. You drink it the same way though. Drop the tonic inside the glitter glass and drink. Quickly." Her eyebrows flick dramatically.

I follow her directions and drop the small glass inside the clear bubbling liquid. Immediately the solutions combine and fizz, rising to the rim at breakneck speed.

"Drink!" Kari calls.

I'm laughing as I put the glass to my lips. It zings

immediately, with a taste not unlike lavender mixed with an exceptionally spicy chai tea. I gulp the concoction down but not before a stream of prickly bubbles escape my mouth, dripping down my chin and onto the floor.

Kari cheers me on and laughs at my failure.

Eyes all around are on us now, but this time, I don't care. Because now, I'm not alone. This time, I'm accepted by someone who belongs.

The pressure on my chest is gone entirely. "Let me show you how it's done." She winks.

She bites her lip as she carefully holds the purple liquid over the clear, pauses, focusing intently, then drops the small glass and chugs like it's a damn race. Maybe it is. She finishes the drink without even one drop escaping her lips.

"Impressive," I say.

"I've had a lot of practice."

This time, a waiter passes by with a drink I recognize. I grab a glass of light red wine that pops like sparkles are inside it.

"Ahh, a wine-y, huh?"

I shrug, brushing that conversation off. I didn't get much time to experience adult drinks in the fae realm. This is literally the only fancy fae drink I'm familiar with, and it's not even from my own court. I know a bit more about wine from the human world, but living as a teenager meant my education was limited to stolen or cheap liqueur. I can make a mean screwdriver, though, and can chug bad whiskey without a wince.

And I'm quite familiar with Yeager bombs.

"Did you spend any time in the human world?" I ask her, now that our antics have settled. I'm honestly glad to have a friend in this crowd of enemies. I don't know why I thought coming to this event could ever be described as a good idea.

I wanted to make a point: that I could belong. Instead, I think I proved the opposite. So far at least. Kari as my drinking partner is helping.

Tyadin would have stuck with me, but I had to go all broody and lost him to hide in the corner like a coward, and now, he's off schmoozing with a few lovely fae ladies.

"One year. Nothing impressive. I rushed a sorority but lost interest quickly. I faked my death in my sophomore year to come back home. That was shortly after my brother died, and I became the new heir to the Crystal Court."

"Oh, I'm sorry."

She waves it off. "We weren't close. He was nearly a hundred years older."

I nod awkwardly, unsure what to say to that.

"So, how's Rev's mission going?" She smiles knowingly.

I shrug. "It's classified."

"So, you're saying you *don't* know anything about it?" She eyes me.

I roll my eyes.

"I'm just curious. Has he made his trip into the Schorchedlands already? I know it's all hush-hush. Most of the world just assumed once a champion was chosen that we were all saved. I know it's a lot more complicated than that."

"I don't know why you think he'd tell me details about it." I watch Rev chatting casually with a group of Glistening Court royals.

Kari smirks. "I was never quite sure what to make of your relationship."

"What do you mean?"

"He's always been obsessed with you. Not in a good way, of course. He talked about killing you so often it got annoying, to be honest. Then once you saved him during the trials..." She pauses. "I don't know, but obviously he changed. A lot."

"It's complicated."

She gives me a half smirk, eyes glistening. "I bet." She watches Rev from across the room too. His eyes dart toward us but then away quickly. "It's too bad your banishment will be reinstated when this is all over."

I purse my lips. I hadn't considered that my presence could be a tell. The only reason my punishment was put on hold was in case Rev failed. It allowed me to continue using resources inside the realm to prepare in case I must take his place inside the Schorchedlands. So, if I'm here, it means there's still a chance Rev can fail.

"You could have found yourself with a crown on your head otherwise," she says.

"What?" I nearly spit my drink out.

She smiles. "As I said, I never quite understood it. But there's one obvious explanation—he's in love with you." She shrugs, her tone so light and casual I can't even comprehend her words.

I choke on my wine. Kari pats my back lazily.

"No... I---What?"

She chuckles, but her face falls back into a serious expression.

"You're insane." I could tell her we're mates. This

magical connection explains all of those things, but it doesn't mean he's in love. It just means all of his feelings about me are strong, whether they're hate or admiration or caring. Love... no. It's definitely not love. "But either way, it doesn't matter."

She nods slowly. "Doomed love. It's tragic."

I spit out a bitter laugh.

"I don't know what happened between you two during the trials, but it became clear it was more than just mutual survival when he healed that girl. It... it didn't make any sense for him to do that unless he cared for you on a deep level."

I bite my lip, eyebrows pulled down low.

"If you knew how much anger he held about his brother's death, about his place in his kingdom... How he didn't trust anyone, not even his closest friends... Well, you'd understand how him being here with you, trusting you with information about the mission that will affect his entire future, his legacy, when he's kept it from everyone else..." She tilts her head. "It paints a pretty clear picture."

"It's... not just me."

"The old Rev would have trusted *no one*."

"I didn't know the old Rev," I say. "I only know the one that's here now."

"Exactly. Because you're the reason for the change."

I shake my head. "You're over-romanticizing this. It's... strange, and... I don't know. But it's just friendship. We're allies."

"He trusts you. Way more than he trusts anyone else. He forgave you for the gravest of sins. How? Why? The only thing that can make me justify that is love."

"He didn't forgive me. How could he? *I* haven't forgiven me." My stomach sinks.

*Your gravest sin. Your deepest seeded flaw.*

*This becomes the soul's new quest.*

I purse my lips as something new occurs to me.

What if she's right? Not about him loving me but about him forgiving me. It seems impossible because... how? How could he forgive me for that? I wouldn't forgive me. I *haven't* forgiven me.

But if it's true—

"Maybe you should ask him." Kari slips away as Rev comes closer, his gentle eyes pinning me in place.

*You have completed your quest.*

What if Rev doesn't belong in the Schorchedlands because, though he's not perfect or too pure, he has achieved the entire purpose of that dark place. What if he faced his own deepest flaw—his hatred of me—and beat it?

What if *forgiveness* was what Rev needed to achieve redemption according to the magical bylaws of fae-hell?

I swallow. If this theory is right, not only am I amazed he'd forgive me but... I am, once again, ruining everything for him. If this theory is right, then I'm the reason Rev can't enter the Schorchedlands.

# 23
## REV

Caelynn is white as a ghost when I approach her. "Are you okay?" I ask softly.

"Fine," she whispers.

Her dress is a lovely cyan, draped gently over her body. My eyes drop to the drink in her hand. A light red wine with sparkles and pops. My eyes narrow as a memory plagues me.

A lovely young fae in a black dress and masquerade mask, unsure what to drink at a Luminescent Court ball. I'd suggested this very drink.

"What?" she asks.

"Nothing." It doesn't much matter. I thought that girl was my mate, and then I'd lost her.

And it was true. I was right all along.

Now, I've met her. I know her. And she's not lacking in anything, except for what she's done. Except that there is no hope for us.

"How do you like the wine?" I ask casually.

"It's good. I've never been much for wine actually."

"More of a tonic lady?"

She smiles, and it tugs on my heart.

"You saw that, huh?"

*I see everything*, I think but don't dare say it. Someday soon Caelynn will be gone. She'll be only a memory. I grab a glass of Callaway wine to match hers. I'd like some things to remind me of her forever. Good things I can hold on to. This wine will be one.

I hold out the glass to her, and she cautiously connects hers with mine in a soft ding.

"To memories," I say.

Her eyebrows pull down in confusion. "What memories?"

I swallow. "This one. When this is all over, I want to have a few things I won't ever forget."

Her face falls slack, amazement, and incredulity and a soft sadness covers her. It's uncharacteristically innocent actually. I want to memorize that too.

Anything but the image of her sadness inside that carriage. The emptiness of her march through the crowd after I'd abandoned her.

"Something they can't take away," I say.

"Something we ourselves can't ruin. It will live forever."

"Now, you get the idea." I smile. "So, tell me, what about this night do you want to remember?"

Her cheeks grow red, and she looks to the floor, but she recovers quickly. "Honestly, I'm just shocked to be here. At the High Court... It's amazing."

"It is, isn't it?"

"I find myself looking for every aspect of my court I can

find," she says, eyes darting around eagerly. "The ceiling, of course, but there's a portrait in the corner of the very first Shadow Court High King. And I'm sure I'm missing more."

I smile, watching her expression. I love her wonder. How her eyes lighten.

"It's just so ironic."

I frown. "What's ironic?"

Her eyes meet mine, the eagerness still there but with a pinch of pain. "That I'd somehow make it *here*, of all places, before my own court's palace."

My eyebrows pull down. "What do you mean?"

"I've never been inside my own court's palace," she admits.

My eyes widen, stomach sinking. "Never?"

She shakes her head. "That was one of my biggest dreams. It's the one part of being a shadow fae that I never completed. Technically speaking, I'm not actually a full citizen. You probably could have used that information to get me kicked out of the trials actually. Now, that I think of it." She laughs, but I'm stuck on her words.

"How have you never been to the palace of your own people?"

She shrugs. "I would have gone in the next year. But it's closed to only the strongest fae in the kingdom because we hardly have enough magic to fuel it, and they're concerned with dilution. They open the gates yearly for one celebration, but only adult fae are allowed. I... well, I never quite made it."

*Never.* She's never been to her own palace. She's a countess, I just assumed... "Is that where you were going before I asked for your help?"

She nods, sadness clear in her eyes though she tries to hide it with a soft smile.

I've met very few people with as much love for their element as Caelynn of the Shadow Court. I remember the look on her face the first moment she set foot back in the Whisperwood, and when the Shadow Sprites welcomed her.

She loves her court, even though she doesn't always agree with them.

Forgetting everything else—the music playing and fae couples twirling to the music, even the queen's judging gaze—I grab Caelynn's hand and pull her out of the ballroom and down an empty hall.

"What are you doing?" she asks.

"Showing you something," I call as I continue my excited walk, pulling her along. She skips after me, huffing in fake annoyance.

Up a set of golden spiral stairs to the second floor and down another wide hall, which ends with a set of massive black doors. Black doors where dark smoke wafts out from the bottom edge.

Caelynn gasps, already recognizing where I've taken her.

I've spent a bit of time in the High Court palace over my years. My family spent a whole week here a month or so before Reahgan was named High Heir. The queen wanted to get to know her potential heirs. There were three families from three different courts as contenders, and each were welcomed guests for a full week.

Apparently, Reahgan had impressed the queen. Although, when a Flicker Court matchmaker declared him

Brielle's mate—well, that certainly helped seal the deal. It was in this palace that they met.

I remember passing this room a dozen times—the inky black magic seeping out from under it eternally—and thinking it was creepy as hell. My brother dared me to go inside because he knew how much it creeped me out. He dragged me down the hall, laughing as he went. Brielle laughed too, though I could tell she was uncomfortable with his forcefulness.

He shoved me into the closed doors and told me he wouldn't let me go back to my own rooms unless I faced my fear and went inside. Reahgan was a strange brother. He loved me, and he was supportive sometimes. But he also loved to showcase his power, especially when there was an audience.

His antics often helped me develop a backbone, though. I relied on him and father too much. So like a mother bird, he shoved me out of the nest... often.

Like in this memory, I refused to whimper and cry—I was an adult fae for God's sake. Young but technically an adult. And I wouldn't be made a fool.

So, I picked myself up and went inside the room of black magic.

Immediately, the shadow magic I feared leaped at me, smothering my screams. I panicked, but as quickly as it enveloped me, it embraced me in a warm welcome. It's strange to feel emotions from magic like that, but its friendliness was so obvious I didn't even question it. The smoky magic settled on my skin like drops of dew, warming my skin.

And it does the same thing the moment Caelynn pulls

open the door. Darkness charges like a stallion and then bathes us in simple warmth and comfort. Caelynn sucks in a breath and I smile.

Ten years ago, I entered this very room terrified of the shadow magic that fueled it only to be amazed at how *beautiful* it was. It was soft and enigmatic.

So much like the shadow fae with me now.

This might become one of my favorite memories ever, watching her eyes glisten as she spins, taking in the room before us. The walls are black stone, the floor appears to be made of black smoke. The ceiling is covered in moving inky magical forms. They're like living silhouettes of creatures and fae, battling and dancing in a lovely ever-changing show.

Against the far wall is a set of windows, freely letting light into the wide-open room. There are dusty chairs and a big table on one end and a dusty fireplace with couches on the other.

"What is this place?" she whispers.

"A meeting room of sorts. It was a gift from Georgio of the Crackling Court, a High King a few hundred years ago. His mate and queen were of the Shadow Court, so he built this place for her."

"Wow," Caelynn breathes. Her eyes are wide in awe as she runs her fingers over the dusty furniture. "It's incredible."

"It's said to have been made in the likeness of the Shadow Palace."

My respect for the Shadow Court went up tenfold the day I first entered this room so long ago; although, it only lasted a few weeks. Because the day a shadow fae assassin slipped into my brother's room and murdered him, my respect turned to acid and ate away at me.

I remember the way the Shadow Court celebrated his death. They were proud of their young assassin. It's one of the reasons I respect Caelynn, despite what she's done— she doesn't relish the act the way I'd expected based on her court's reaction.

They painted her to be a hero. Like killing a young fae was something to be revered. But she doesn't. She hates what she did. And she hates the way they romanticize it.

*She did it for me.*

"It's incredible, Rev," she says, her voice breathy. "They're phantoms, a relation of the shadow sprites." She watches the forms on the ceiling.

"They're living creatures?" I ask. I hadn't realized. But then, this room always had felt alive.

She nods. "They won't speak to you directly the way the sprites occasionally do, but they send messages by playing an act. Visitors in the Whisperwood have often said that monsters hunted them, chasing them away from the proper path. Or that there were entire villages of shadow people hiding in the forest. But they are the phantoms. Playing tricks on travelers, or helping, depending on their mood."

I look up at their moving forms. "What do you think their mood is now?"

A soft hum begins from above us, a gentle beat. Then, the forms shift into a clear image. A couple dancing. Caelynn chuckles. "It's a waltz."

I smile. "I think they want us to dance."

Our eyes meet, and my smile fades as her lips part.

She's hypnotizingly beautiful. I find myself begging for any way to undo the past. For some way for this, us, to be right.

I suppose it can be here in this moment, with no one around to judge us. With no expectations of what tomorrow may bring.

A temporary dream.

My heart aches and soars at the same time as I hold out my hand. She takes it, her skin zinging against mine, warming my blood in the same way the welcoming dark magic of this room did.

I decide quickly, if I do become king of this palace one day, I'm going to fix up this room and revive it. I'll be able to feel her here. She'll be with me every moment I spend here, even when she's far, far away.

I pull her in close, throwing the true form of a waltz out the window, and press our bodies together. She lets out another gasp, and my head spins with desire.

If this moment is all we have, I'll live it to the fullest.

We spin together, rocking and twirling to the gentle beat of the phantoms above. They dance with us—Caelynn and I, together in the way we were always meant to be.

Light and dark. Push and pull. Love and hate.

Caelynn licks her lips, and it does something to me, aching deep down in my bones. I swallow, and we slow to a stop.

Her breath is shallow as we stand there beneath the phantoms, who continue their dance. Her heaving chest is pressed against mine. I have one hand at her back and the other at her shoulder, her skin tingling beneath my fingertips.

I reach for a strand of her hair that curls over her shoulder, loosened from its binds, and I rub it beneath my fingers.

She doesn't move, and neither do I. For minutes, we stand there together.

Her eyes dart up to the ceiling, where the silhouette of two large faces appear. Slowly, they approach each other until they connect in a gentle kiss.

Caelynn smirks. "Matchmakers tonight, are you?"

But they're not wrong. Caelynn and I are like two magnets. Opposites, who cannot help but drift together. I stop fighting it, this pull, and I lean in. Her eyes widen. She pauses, her breath tickling my jaw.

Then, she jerks forward fiercely pressing her lips to mine.

I fall into her like gravity. I grip her tightly and take her bottom lip between my teeth. She gasps and then moans—a sound I am certain will forever haunt my dreams.

Caelynn grips my suit jacket in a tight fist and jerks me forward so that I fall with her onto the small platform at the front of the room. Her legs wrap around my waist, and I press harder into her.

I live in this moment, hand on the back of her head, fist in her hair as we explore each other in so many of the ways we'd fantasied. Her mouth opens for me, and I oblige, pressing deeper. I want her. All of her. Every inch.

Her nails dig into my neck, and I groan. My mind spinning, body burning.

The thought of living without her, without this, is unbearable.

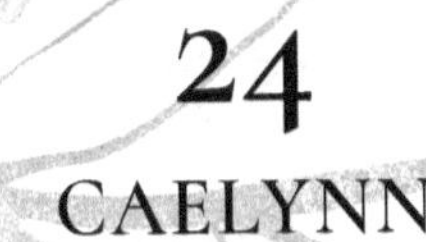

# 24
## CAELYNN

Footsteps sound behind us, and the shadow creatures above hiss. Rev pulls back and turns to face the doorway where the king of the Luminescent Court stands, backed by several Luminescent Guards.

Rev stands between us protectively, his hand still entwined with mine.

"What are you doing here, Father?" he asks, with a bitter bite to the words.

"I suppose I shouldn't be surprised," the king says, spitting onto the smoking ground, his lip curled in disgust. My stomach sinks. But Rev has not yet let my hand go.

The ceiling hisses and grumbles in annoyance. The phantoms are not fans of their new visitors.

"You here, with your Shadow Court whore."

Rev's jaw clenches, and he moves to step forward, but I grip his hand tightly, not allowing him to leave me behind. "He's baiting you," I warn.

"I always knew you were a disappointment," the arrogant king continues, his eyes dark. "But I hadn't imagined you'd disgrace your brother this way. I underestimated your pathetic nature."

"You know nothing, Father."

"Don't you dare call me that!" He marches forward. His guards follow closely behind. "If you think I won't expose your secret of dirty blood..."

"You've had thirty years to expose it. Why would you do it now?"

"Because of her!" he says, veins bulging. "If you think I'll let you pardon her, or make her a queen, I will tear down everything I've built. I will burn the world to the ground before I let that happen."

I clench my jaw, anger simmering in my belly. But at the same time, I understand him. I hate myself with that same rage sometimes.

"You're wrong about her," Rev says, and I close my eyes, soaking those words in. I want this to be right. I want so badly not to have to do what comes next.

Because Rev is wrong about me. He believes in me. He cares for me.

And even though I can't even comprehend it, he's forgiven me for an unforgivable act.

The king laughs, throwing his head back, his eyes black as the walls around us. "You think you know her, do you? She's an opportunist, you fool. Nothing more. She uses her beauty to manipulate. Why else do you think she was in your brother's room the day she killed him? When he rejected her, she turned on him."

Rev rolls his eyes. "You have no idea what you're—"

"No, YOU have no idea," he screams, and everything hushes, even the phantoms above.

My blood runs cold.

"You don't know who she is, who she works for." He prowls forward. "That creature—he doesn't let go of his pets."

I pull in a breath. He knows about the Night Bringer.

"He keeps them and continues to force them to his will. And he chooses them well. She's an evil creature's minion, and you're *in love* with her."

I pull my hand from Rev's and take a shaky step back. He's wrong. I'm not working for the Night Bringer anymore. But how did he know?

"Do you know how I found her?" the king asks.

Rev can't take his eyes off of the man he still calls father, even though he knows better. Is he beginning to believe him? Good.

My stomach sinks, pain washing over me. It's good if he learns to hate me again. It will make all of this easier.

"After she killed your brother, do you know what she did? She *laughed*."

I suck in a breath.

"She LAUGHED," he yells through the hushed room. "Hysterically. Over his cold body. That's the woman you chose to warm your bed."

Rev freezes. I can't see his face, because I'm a damn coward still standing behind him, but his muscles tense, and his father's face calms, smoothing into a smug look like he knows he got to him. My breath comes out shaky.

"She liked it," the Luminescent Court king says slowly, calmly. "She enjoyed killing him."

"No," Rev breathes. "It's not true."

"Ask her."

Slowly, Rev turns to face me and tears well in my eyes. Because his father is right in a way. I did laugh when I killed Reahgan. Not exactly for the reasons he's implying. I didn't relish the death of another fae. I didn't enjoy killing.

But Rev doesn't know what his brother was really like.

But even though Reahgan was a dick of the worst kind, even that wasn't why I'd laughed. No, it was because I'd won.

I was stuck in an impossible situation between giving myself away to permanent slavery to a sadistic ancient beast or killing my mate—the sweet and good-hearted Rev. I found a loophole in the bargain. I broke free of his clutches and saved us both by killing Reahgan, a power-hungry fae who enjoyed causing pain.

He threatened to torture me, implied terrible, sick things he'd do to me before he killed me slowly. And when I used the magic given to me by the Night Bringer to turn the tides back on Reahgan, the weak Shadow Court fae he taunted, I won both battles. I killed Reahgan, my tormentor. And beat the Night Bringer, my would-be master.

And it felt good.

I could tell Rev all of this. I could explain it... and maybe he'd believe me. Maybe it would be enough.

Maybe, just maybe, we'd go back to how things were just moments ago.

But what then?

He needs to get inside the Schorchedlands or lose his inheritance. Lose his place in his own court. Lose his chance to be High King.

And his father already said he'd do anything to make sure I'm never pardoned. And I believe him. There's so much still hanging over my head. The chances of being together with all of this between us are so small it's hardly visible.

I'm not Cinderella. Not a princess. Not the hero. I will never have my happily ever after.

But there are some things I can achieve. I can give Rev what he needs to achieve his true destiny—become the savior of the realm and High King.

All he has to do is hate me again, and he can have it all. He can enter the Schorchedlands and become the hero he's meant to be.

He and I... we've always been doomed. So, maybe I can choose him again. Maybe I can play this role that I've become so good at one more time, and I can give him everything that he needs.

*Hate me, Rev. I'm sorry, but you have to hate me.*

"It's true," I say, my voice still wobbly. But I pull in all my determination and push away all the pain. "They found me laughing over his body."

Rev's jaw drops, and I hate myself. His darkened eyes fill with tears, even as his jaw clenches. Already, I see the old Rev. The Rev at the beginning of the trials that vowed to kill me. Cruel and wounded.

That's the Rev that will save us all.

But I hate it. I hate every second of it.

"I loved it," I say, my voice steadier now, though my heart trembles, my soul crumbles inside. I just have to hide it from him. "Reahgan was an arrogant dick that deserved what he got."

Rev jerks back like I slapped him.

"I laughed because it felt good. Ending his life.

Watching his lips go blue. I'd do it again if given the chance, and I'd enjoy it just as much."

My eyes flash to Rev's father, who is one part appalled, one part pleased. He, unlike me, enjoys Rev's pain. My focus is still on the Luminescent King when Rev charges me.

He screams in agony but finds only smoke as I twist away and disappear into shadow. The phantoms reach down and clasp me, welcoming me into their arms, and I join them in the smoke hovering above the room.

Now, I look down at them all, like this is really a show. It's a scene playing out and not my life. It's only pretend, my heart shattering.

Dark and comforting magic keeps me hidden. I wonder if I could stay here forever. Just like I'd hoped I could stay in the Whisperwood for the rest of my life. No one would find me here. They'd think I'd just vanished. Ran away.

Rev falls to his knees where I had just stood, chest heaving. Part of me hopes he'd seen through my act. He's seen me. The real me.

His father stalks toward him and squats, leaning down to his ear. "You always were a fool, Reveln," he whispers loudly. "And now, a complete failure. It will be easy to disinherit you now that you're the failed savior." He chuckles and retreats from the room, leaving Rev on his hands and knees.

He stays there, hands clenched in his hair, unmoving, for another full minute as I grapple with the intense desire to drop down and comfort him. Beg him to forgive me. Explain to him all of it, tell him I lied—I didn't relish Reahgan's death, and I certainly don't relish his pain now.

Finally, Rev stands and marches from the room.

I hop down from my hiding place with the phantoms. Shadowy arms reach out for me, and I sigh.

"I know," I whisper. "I'm—" putting on a show. Playing a part. And for the rest of my life, I'll be a phantom. "Just like you."

# 25

## CAELYNN

I give myself one more minute to mourn and pull myself together.

Still unsure I made the right choice but... I had to do it, right? The opportunity to push him away met us, and I couldn't turn it down because it was what he needed. Even if he doesn't know it. Even if he'll never know it.

My heart shatters, realizing he'll never know that what I did was for him.

He will hate me forever, and I did it on purpose.

Nausea roils through my gut, but I clench my jaw, steeling myself against the pain. Using it to my advantage.

This is my punishment for the truth in those words. They weren't all lies, the way I wish they were.

I did enjoy killing Reahgan. And I would do it again.

I'd do anything to save Rev, no matter how much it hurt both of us.

I pull in a long breath and then march from the room. I rush back down the hall Rev had led me, and I slip through the crowds in the grand hall, shadows hiding me from notice. Up the stairs and back out to the Crumbling Court carriage in line among the other high court vessels.

Killian, Rev's stag huffs, and shuffles as I approach.

I slip inside the carriage door and ruffle through the storage compartment. Rev has a bag set for a trip into the Schorchedlands, just in case. Well, tonight, if my plan works, he'll be using it.

I grab the leather backpack and turn to find a very serious dwarfish fae watching me.

"What are you doing?" Tyadin asks, his arms crossed.

I hop from the carriage and shove the bag into his arms. "Good, just the person I need."

His eyebrows pull down as he examines the bag in his arms. "What's this?" he asks. "And what the hell is going on? Rev is flipping out."

"I need you to trust me," I say with a weak voice. "Can you do that? Can you trust me?"

"Yes. But that doesn't answer the question."

I clench my teeth tightly. "I did what I had to. Just... Okay look, Rev needs to go to the Schorchedlands. Now. Tonight. But he won't go on my prompting. I need you to take the bag to him and tell him to head there now."

Tyadin pauses, examining me. He shakes his head, disbelief covering his features.

"Please," I beg. "I figured it out. I fixed it. He can go now. But he'll never trust me again. So, I need you to do it. And don't tell him it was from me. That's important. He can't know I had anything to do with it."

Tyadin presses his eyes closed in a wince. "Okay," he says. Then, he turns on his heel and treks back into the ballroom with Rev's leather bag in hand.

# 26
## REV

I take a shot of tonic and then another.

"Whoa there."

I ignore the voice, not remotely caring who is speaking or what they have to say. The only thing I can think is— the only thing I'll *let* myself think—how to send my mind to oblivion. I want to be so drunk I don't remember this night.

Not one dammed moment of it.

A delicate hand pops over the top of my next drink, purple nails glittering up at me.

"You okay, Rev?" Kari asks.

"No," I growl.

"Okay, then," she says, grabbing the drink from my hand and tossing it down her own throat.

"That was mine," I say between gritted teeth.

"The scourge is lying in wait just outside the village I was born in," Kari says casually. As if it wasn't major, terrifying news. "It hasn't moved in two weeks. I'm grateful for that." She grabs two glasses of sparkling champagne and hands me one. "But I'm terrified of the moment it resumes its journey. We've evacuated the villages closest, but we can never predict where it will turn next." She takes a small sip of her sparkling drink. "I don't want it to kill my people, Rev."

A shiver runs down my spine. "I don't either," I whisper.

"So, if there's something wrong—if you need something—I will do whatever it takes to help you defeat this enemy. Okay? I won't tell anyone you don't want me to. I will give you any aid you require with no questions asked. Do you understand?"

I swallow, blinking rapidly. The reminder of my imminent quest, the fate of my entire world on my shoulders has me sobered up quick as hell.

"I'll ask again," she says after a small sip of her glass. "Are you okay?" She meets my eye directly for the first time.

"No," I say. I'm falling apart. And I don't know how to stop it.

"What do you need?" Her eyes are sharp, expression fierce. She's ready to tear the world down to save her people.

*I don't know.* I don't voice the thought because I can't admit that. I need to feel something other than the pain raging through me now.

A rough hand grabs my shoulder and whips me to face him.

"What the hell, Ty."

He shoves a bag into my hands. "You have to go."

I blink. "What?" I grip the leather strap of the backpack in my hands. It's mine. My supplies for the Schorchedlands I'd brought along for no other reason than it made me feel better.

"It's time to go," he says, punctuating each word. "Trust me." His eyes are sharp, as serious as I've ever seen him.

"You're sure?" I ask him, my heart pounding. I'm eager for it to be true for so many reasons at once. Honestly, my biggest reason is for something to take my mind off of... what happened with my father just minutes ago.

My stomach turns.

My heart pounds faster. "Go, now?" I repeat again, stupidly.

"Yes!" he says and shoves at my shoulder.

I don't understand any of it, but then again, I'm not in my right mind. A bottle of water is shoved into my hand, and I turn to meet Kari's purple eyes. "Drink it. And if you need anything... my offer stands."

I nod in thanks and then march through the crowd and out the door without looking back.

Up the stairs, I glance back only once to see the queen watching me, narrow eyes, and almost—displeased? I shake it off, my head still somewhat dizzy, but I'm determined. Determined to run from all of this. My not-father's disappointment and disgust. The people's hope that I'll save them all. The prying questions. And most importantly, Caelynn.

Killian whinnies and huffs as I approach him. I unclip

him from the carriage and hop onto his back saddleless. It'll be an uncomfortable ride, but it'll do.

I hope to God I never see her face again as long as I live, and if Tyadin is right, that something has changed and I can get through the Wicked Gates, I'll never have to.

# 27
## CAELYNN

My back is pressed to the wall, knees against my chest, as I watch the fae royals mosey out of the High Court palace and to their carriages. No one notices me, hidden in the shadows. My dress has streaks of mud up the skirt. My eyes are red and itchy.

Another set of fae walk down the fairy-lit walkway but stop to look around.

"There," a feminine voice says.

I blink to see Tyadin and Kari crossing the snow-covered grounds to meet me at the edge of the front entryway.

Kari sits beside me and throws an arm over my shoulder. My heart squeezes, and I press into her warmth.

"Are you going to tell me what happened now?"

I blink and stare down at my frozen toes, shoes lost to some bush I attacked in my pained outrage. I only have myself to blame.

With Kari here, I'm not sure if I should explain, but I don't have the energy to think much beyond that. I trust her. Maybe it's stupid. Maybe it'll backfire. But it's not like I could make Rev trust me any less at this point.

"The Schorchedlands has a purpose," I say mechanically, my soul lost to the wind. "*It is not for the unredeemable. It's for the unredeemed.*"

Tyadin purses his lips. "What does that mean?"

"It means anyone can be redeemed," Kari says, eyebrows pulled down in concentration.

I nod. "The Schorchedlands allows evil spirits the chance to achieve what they couldn't on earth. But they don't need to be perfect. They only need to resolve their biggest conflict. The one thing that held them back. The *largest blot on their soul*, one of the books called it."

"Okay?" Tyadin says.

"Rev had already resolved his."

Tyadin takes in a long breath and finally sits beside me. I get the feeling he didn't have the energy to continue standing.

"The Schorchedlands wouldn't let him in," Kari breaths, putting all the pieces together now.

"How?" Ty asks, ignoring Kari's realization and getting right to the point.

"He forgave me," I whisper, and my heart breaks all over again.

Kari goes dead still, arm still tight around me.

"So, you undid it," Ty says, his voice harsh.

"I made him hate me again." I nod. I suck in a shaky breath. "His father cornered us and made accusations about me. I just agreed with him. They were partially true anyway. I just... said what I knew would hurt him the most."

"Wow," Kari breathes. "Are you sure it worked?"

I nod.

"We won't know for sure until the morning," Tyadin says.

"It worked," I say. "I can feel it. He'll be inside within the hour."

Kari shakes her head in disbelief.

I don't respond. I can't. I'd lose it if I affirmed her words anyway.

"I'm so sorry, Cae."

Tyadin rests his hand on my forearm. "I'll tell him. When he returns with the cure, I'll make sure he knows what you did and why."

I force a smile through my tears. "Thanks," I say. But I know it won't matter. Rev is gone for good. And there's nothing anyone else could do to take it back.

# 28
## REV

The thorn wall towers over me, making my path nearly impossible to see in the depth of shadows. I rode Killian straight through the Luminescent portal, out the gates of the place I grew up in—the place she betrayed me. The place I lost my brother. Through the iridescent forest and the portal to the base of the Wicked Gates.

Pain and rage still eat away at me as I pull Killian to a stop. My limbs feel tingly, and I know I'm not in the best state to do this. Those last few shots have wormed their way into my bloodstream, and I'm feeling the full brunt of the hallucinogens. But I have to do this now.

I don't know why I'm here. My mind spins, and I stumble as I hop from Killian's back. Why is this supposed to be different? Because I hate her now? Because I'm eager for her to be re-banished.

"Let me in, stupid wall!" I shout and run forward into the thorn nook. I duck my head as I enter. Stupid place. I hate this door, so snarky and rude every time I try to pass through. "I'm just trying to save the whole world," I grumble.

Without pausing to think, I pull out my knife and swipe it across my palm and slam it to the nob where my blood is supposed to go.

*You again,* the voice hisses. But then, there's a hum, low and inhuman.

"Let me in," I say, my anger swirling, soul as black as hers. "Just FUCKING OPEN THE DOOR," I scream.

Suddenly, there's a click and the vines shudder.

*Well, what a surprise. Your soul is welcomed, Reveln,* the voice purrs at me. *You may enter. But you, and only you, will be permitted to exit through this gate without achieving redemption—if you live. If you die within these walls, you will be as any other wraith—unable to leave until you have achieved your quest. If you die, another may take your place.*

My heart pounds. *It's letting me in?*

*Fuck.* Ty was right.

My stomach twists, my heart aches, and my mind spins. I clench my fists tightly as the vines before me untangle, leaving an opening just large enough for me to walk through. *This is it.*

I will either die a failure or live a hero.

Past the opening is pitch black. I can't see a single thing. "Thank you," I say calmly, though my heart throbs wildly.

And then, I step into hell.

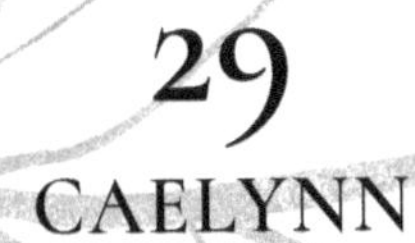

# 29
## CAELYNN

Raindrops begin to fall, sending water streaming down my arms, chilling my body. Kari and Tyadin left me not long ago to head back inside and say their proper goodbyes, but I'm not alone long. Footsteps approach slowly and then stop a few feet away.

"Pathetic creature." The Luminescent Court's King's voice chills me. "I hear my son has finally ventured to the Schorchedlands."

My eyes flit up to his. His expression is blank. How would he know what Rev is doing? He wasn't even supposed to know he hadn't been able to enter.

His silver eyes shine, and his lip quirks like he's fighting a smile. I shiver, eyes locked with his, panic filling me. Something is wrong with this fae. Something... isn't right.

My heart starts pounding harder.

"I'll certainly be glad to be rid of the bastard."

I grimace but don't speak.

"I'm surprised by your reputation. I expected you to be a much more challenging opponent. The only fae to ever outsmart the Night Bringer." He shakes his head, and I leap to my feet, hands in fists.

He laughs harder, and a soft glow appears between us. He's blocking me from attacking him. My chest heaves. He knows. How much does he know? My eyes flit over him then stop dead on a thorn tattoo on his wrist.

My blood runs ice cold, my vision tinges with black. I barely hear his condescending tone as he continues talking to me. I don't need to hear his words; I already know what happened.

"Only a few of us know, of course. But those with any knowledge of the ancient being can tell. That power of yours? That magic you showcased during the final trial? Like flaunting it in his face. You weren't supposed to get away, did you know that?"

"I don't know what you're talking about." My voice is hoarse. But I do. I know exactly what he's talking about.

For these few moments, I'm back there. A terrified teenage fae, trembling in that ancient beast's presence. He made me think he was down one cave so that I'd flee straight toward him in another.

He likes to make one think they're in control. He likes to herd fae. Scare them in one direction only to find out that's exactly where he wants them.

"Anyway," the king says offhandedly. "You were easier to manipulate than I expected. The Night Bringer has plans for the boy, and I have mine. Both of them are nicely achieved by him entering those cursed walls. We were all quite miffed when the wall refused to allow him entrance. I'd wondered if another ancient was in play and altered the magic of the gates, but once he saw how close you two had gotten, our master figured it out for himself and sent me to do what I do best. Hurt Reveln. And oh, how you helped so nicely."

My mind spins, vision blinking black.

*Our master.*

"He's not my master," I spit.

He chuckles. "Just because you can't see his chains on your wrists doesn't mean you're not playing on his team."

I swallow.

"I still hate you for what you did to my true heir." He spits into the fresh snow between us. "Reahgan was my son. My heir. The perfect legacy. And you stole him from me." He heaves in a huge breath. "But time dulls the sting." He lets the breath out. "Now, my only desire is to destroy the changeling living in my true son's place."

"You could just expose the truth about him." I cross my arms. "Instead, you'd do the bidding of that creature?"

He chuckles. "Sometimes, you must take terrible allies to get what you desire. Rev understood that when he took your side. You didn't really think he cared for you, did you? You're a convenient ally and easy on the eyes. Any affection you think he holds was only the bond magic. I did you a favor. He was never going to take you as a bride. You're not worthy of him, and he knows it." He laughs. "And that's coming from me! I hate him and still know he's better than you."

My stomach twists.

"Doesn't matter, though. You've helped ensure his death. For that, I should thank you." The look in his eye tells me he most definitely does not feel grateful.

"You underestimate him."

"Oh, no, sweetheart. He might have been able to retrieve the cure—if that were even a thing." He shakes his head, chuckling darkly.

"What does that mean?"

"It means, *my lovely pet.*" My knees almost buckle at those words. I shake my head, tears of frustration in my eyes. "That this game is much larger than the scourge."

*I'm not a child anymore*, I tell myself. And this arrogant king is giving me information freely because he enjoys watching me squirm. I am squirming. I'm freaking the fuck out. My chest hurts, my head spins, my fingertips are tingling. But I have to keep him talking as long as I can. He thinks he's won this game, and so he'll spill everything here and now.

My teeth chatter. "What did you do?" My voice trembles.

"Nothing extraordinary." He shrugs. "Just ensured that Reveln will perish inside those wicked walls. If he gets past the first few obstacles, he will have about ten thousand wraiths hunting him. How long do you think he will last? If he makes it through Death Valley, I'd be shocked. But even if he does, he will not survive even a moment past the fires."

I mark his words carefully. He's giving me a road map, even if I don't know exactly what they mean.

"Then, Rev will be dead, and you'll have your chance to prove yourself and save the realm. What *he* does with you —I don't much care. Will he let you have your reward now that you helped end Reveln's life after all?" He strokes his chin.

I groan as another wave of pain wracks through my body.

He smiles, his silver eyes glinting with dark wickedness.

"Reveln, the fraud prince, is now exactly where the Night Bringer wants him."

# 30
## CAELYNN

I don't wait for another word from the evil king of the Luminescent Court. If I'd spent one more moment with him, I'd have attacked him—no matter the consequences.

There is a simple truth ringing through my brain.

Rev just walked straight into a trap set by his father, who is working for the Night Bringer. Nausea rolls through me. I can't... God, I can't let this happen.

I fought so hard to free myself and Rev from *his* evil clutches. I gave up everything so that we could live. And now... now he's found a new way to carve my heart out. By killing the fae I love.

These truths add up to one obvious course of action. I must go to the Schorchedlands—now. The Night Bringer is targeting Rev.

I won't let him face this alone. Maybe if there's two of us... we can defeat our enemies.

I rummage through the supplies in the carriage. There's not much here. A knife, a scarf, a few potions. No extra clothes, which is what I really need. I'm not sure I can survive that place without a sturdy pair of boots at the very least.

"What are you doing?"

I spin to face Tyadin and Kari. "Looking for supplies."

Ty's eyes narrow. "What kind of supplies?"

"I need boots," I say, turning back and looking through the near-empty storage container like I'll find something new where there obviously isn't anything.

"Why would you need boots?" His voice is strained, almost like he already knows the answer and he's just hoping he's wrong.

I pause and have a few calming breaths before I face them.

"Rev's father set him up."

"What?" Ty and Kari say at the same time.

"He's working with..." My eyes flit to Kari and back to Ty. I've told her a lot, but I won't trust her with that information. Even Tyadin knows very little. "Someone really bad. And they've set a trap for him. They're going to kill him there. He won't ever come back... unless."

"Unless what?" Ty says, stepping forward. He reaches out and grabs my upper arm tightly, his eyes sharp, grasping mine. "Whatever it is, you can't stop it."

"Don't say that," I spit. "You don't know what I can do."

"It's too late," he whispers. "He'll be well into the Schorchedlands before you reach him. You can't stop him from entering..."

"I wasn't planning to stop him. I'm planning to save him."

"You're going to enter the Schorchedlands after him?" Kari whispers, pity clear in her eyes, followed by judgment. "In a *dress*."

"I was looking for other clothes," I say defensively.

She shakes her head. "You need more than boots. You need real supplies."

Ty spins on Kari. "You're NOT encouraging this."

Kari purses her lips. "I'm just saying that if..."

"No!" Tyadin roars. "No ifs! Caelynn," he turns on me, fury and pain in his eyes, "if you enter now only one of you can leave."

My stomach twists. "Yes," I whisper.

"You're committing suicide."

"No."

"Yes, that's what you're doing. Because you're headed there to save him. And if you succeed, you'll never be able to leave. Ever."

I bite my lip. "You act as if that's a problem."

His hand flies at me, and I flinch, expecting a fist, but his open palm presses against my chest until my back slams against the carriage. "No!" he roars at me. "You matter, Caelynn. I will not let you throw your life away like it doesn't matter!"

"What's the alternative, Ty?" I yell back. His hand still presses against my chest, suppressing a breath, but no part of me feels threatened. "If he lives, I'm banished to the human world. Is it really so different than being banished to the Schorchedlands?"

"Yes! In the human world, you can have a life! You can find happiness."

I shake my head, tears falling freely now. "Everything

—EVERYTHING—was for Rev. Every sacrifice I ever made. Every terrible thing I did. Every choice. It was all for him. If he dies—it was all for nothing. If the Night Bringer gets to him now, then he won." My lips curl into a snarl, anger, and magic clenching inside of me. "I will not let him win!" I yell.

Kari gasps, eyes wide, but she doesn't respond. What does she know of the Night Bringer? I'd never heard of him before he forced me into a bargain, but I'm wondering if his legend isn't as obscure as I'd once thought. Is he well known among the ruling courts? Are there legends I'd never heard of?

"If Rev dies, I go into the Schorchedlands anyway. If I go now, we can fight together and increase our chances of defeating an enemy that I know firsthand is near impossible to defeat. We need to be together, or you can guarantee you lose us both. Even if I go now and Rev survives, then I simply traded one form of banishment for another."

The pressure on my chest lessens, but Ty doesn't pull his hand back. Tears well in his eyes. "I can't let you do this."

I curl my fingers around the hand over my heart and squeeze. "I love you too, Ty." I give him a sad smile. "But I have to do it."

He closes his eyes and shakes his head softly, his shoulders sag in defeat.

"You're willing to run off on some impossible mission," I say softly, "which will likely result in your death, for the off chance you can help re-establish a nation for your forgotten people. Is this so different?"

"Yes," he whispers, eyes cast to the ground. I know I've

already won the argument, but he continues, "Because there's hope, even if it's small. If you go now, there is no hope. You're lost, without any doubt."

"I know you don't realize it," I say. "But I was lost a really long time ago."

He shakes his head. "You're wrong." His fierce eyes meet mine again. "You think you're a lost soul, destroyed in that battle ages ago. But you are the absolute strongest person I've ever met. Your soul may be scarred. You might have pain. Your magic may be one of darkness. But you, Caelynn of the Shadow Court, are bright as the fucking sun."

My mouth falls open as I examine his face. He believes it.

"It was only a matter of time," he says more gently. "Rev saw it too. It was hard for him, but he was falling in love with you. He'd have loved you. And he'd have found a way to free you, eventually. I saw it. That future, where you could have been together. You could have been happy. I wanted that for you."

I press my eyes closed, my lip trembles. "I couldn't see it," I admit. "But I wanted it too."

Ty's hand falls from my chest, freeing me.

I stand there, heaving in breaths, pain pressing down on me. Then, finally, I sniff and stand up straight, determination filling me again.

"Choice is up to you, Cae," Kari says. "Are you staying or going?" She's not trying to push me one way or the other.

"I'm going." There's no doubt.

She nods sharply. "Then come with me."

My chin jerks back. "What? Where?"

"My court is one portal away. I'll get you set up with all the supplies you need and send you on your way."

I blink slowly. I have plenty of things in the Crumbling Court, but that's an hour's ride away. "Okay, then."

I give Ty a long hug and thank him for everything. His friendship, his aid, his belief in me. All of it means the world. Then, I follow Kari toward a black stallion, eyeing us.

"For the record, I agree with everything Ty said just now."

"Uhh, thanks, I guess?" Much of what he said was saying I shouldn't go. Does she mean that too? Because she's being rather supportive if so.

"But I'd do the same thing if I were in your position, and I'd destroy anyone who stood in my way. I don't intend to be that person."

"Thank you."

# 31
## REV

The wind howls, blowing over my skin and tossing my hair wildly. Luckily, it's just barely long enough to reach my eyes. I ignore the occasional sting and continue pressing into the roaring wind.

The air here is at least twenty degrees colder than the other side of the wall and much too dark to see.

If I'd thought this through, I'd have slept the night in that tame forest before entering the Schorchedlands. But I couldn't think anything through before.

I still can't think very clearly, if I'm honest. Rage still devours me from the inside out. Pain I couldn't possibly explain presses down on me.

Her voice rings in my ears.

Caelynn telling me how she's enjoyed murdering my brother. I shake my head. How had I ever let her get that close? How had I ever trusted her?

Bile rises in my throat. Never again.

Now that I'm here, I'll never have to see her again.

Now, I'm here, and I simply have to deal with what's ahead. I'll focus on this mission and nothing more. She can't hurt me again.

The world before me is so dark I can barely see where I'm stepping. How am I supposed to find a place to camp for the night if I can't even see what's around me?

There's a faint clinking and the groan of pained spirits in the distance. They're far off, though. Not a direct threat.

The ground here is soft and mushy, and as I march forward, it only gets worse. Soon my boots are sinking into the muck with each step. If it gets any worse, I'll have to turn back, seeking firmer ground. I could easily get stuck in mud this thick. And that's assuming this is simple mud I'm dealing with. I'm in the Schorchedlands, I remind myself, and the muck very well may be cursed or poisoned or alive. Many unpleasant options.

I blink, trying to will my eyes to focus in the darkness. No such luck. My fingers and lips are still numb, my brain a bit fuzzy. I won't be entirely sober for a few hours still—all the more reason I should sleep.

Something pinches my shin, and I jerk back, only to wince at another sharp jab to the back of my thigh. I freeze and brush at my thigh. Something pinches my fingers, and I pull away a briar. Wonderful.

I groan and attempt a gentle reversal of my steps. I turn and retreat until I find my boots are on solid ground. Not entirely dry or firm but better.

The wind groans in my ear again; only this time, it sends a shiver down my spine. More groans fill the air.

That... is not the wind.

Phantoms. Wraiths. Cursed souls. That's what populates this place. They're not all fae but also animals and creatures whose souls couldn't pass on to the beyond.

I pull out my iron blade. It's dull, but it's not the blade itself that will protect me. Iron can cut even through spirits. This small blade and my magic, those are my only real weapons against the inhabitants of this place.

While the spirits here don't care one way or another if I retrieve the cure—they will kill anyone who gets too close, and they are especially annoyed with living beings impeding their eternal restless punishment. There are traps set every step of the way, looking to ensnare souls—living or non. They don't care.

My heart beats louder, and I press closer to the edge of the thorn walls. Not exactly the ideal place to camp because if you roll too close, you may find a foot-long thorn slicing through your body easier than a sword. But I also know journeying through the Schorchedlands blind is a terrible idea. The closer to the center I get, the more dangerous it becomes. After walking the perimeter for a short while, I'm able to find a small copse of trees. I can't tell what kind, but they'll provide enough cover to act as a shelter for the next few hours.

The howl of a wolf, or something like it, calls in the distance, followed by several more groans and cries. I pull my thin blanket from my pack and throw it over my shoulders as lean my back against the tree, sliding to the ground.

I close my heavy eyes.

I'm here. I made it. The path ahead won't be easy, but I can now focus on my quest.

*I'm not a failure*, I remind myself. Not yet.

In the morning, I'll begin my long trek across these cursed lands and find a way to reach my destiny. For now, I've just got to survive until the morning.

# 32
## CAELYNN

Equipped with a new leather ensemble, several weapons and potions, and a backpack full of supplies, I ride my new shiny, bright-white steed through the forest toward the Schorchedlands.

Luckily, the horse Kari let me borrow isn't afraid of portals—the way Rev's stag had been—because I've traveled through several to get here. After our stop in the Crystal Court, I rode my new steed back through the portal to the High Court, then through the Luminescent Court portal—the faces of those Luminescent guards were priceless—and then, finally, through the iridescent forest and to the portal that dropped me a mile north of the Wicked Gates. It sounds like a far way to travel, but it only took minutes. My horse hardly broke a sweat.

The pathway is dark, but I have no problem navigating ahead, and the filly is confident in my abilities. I quite like this horse actually. White isn't my preferred color, but its confident gate and smooth stride is enough to make up for that shortfall. Besides, anyone, creature or person, who trusts me is welcome in my book.

The Wicked Gate towers over us, and I slow my horse to a trot until we're directly below it. I hop off of her and pat her neck. "Thank you for an easy and pleasant ride." I turn and look at the thorn wall before me. "Part of me wishes I could take you with me."

The horse whinnies and stomps.

"Oh, hush. I'm not really going to. I know better than that."

She snorts, and I laugh.

"I like you because you trusted me," I tell her, rubbing her nose. I have no idea how much she understands. Many fae-realm creatures are significantly more intelligent than their human-world counterparts. In fact, rumor has it that animals here were once fae who transformed themselves into animals and became trapped. Still, I don't have much experience with fae-realm animals to know how much of that is true. All I know is she seems to understand, and so, I'll treat her as if she can. "I wouldn't reward that trust by dooming you to the fate I'm dooming myself." My face falls at that thought. I sniff and stand up straighter. "Kari will send someone for you in the morning. Don't go far," I tell her.

And then, I approach the magical gate before me.

The usually bright green wall of vines and thorns is dark and shadowed. I swear the vines shift and slither like snakes in places—but the moment I look, they freeze in their place. Or maybe it's just my imagination.

I step into the small nook, shrinking beneath the imposing thorns pointing directly down at my head.

Pointer finger out, I reach up toward one of the points—is it as sharp as it looks?

The vine over my head hisses.

I flinch. "What?" I ask as if the wall was sentient. I suppose it could be based on the way it treated Rev.

A faint chuckle rumbles through the whole wall around me. The thorns wiggle over me, and I squirm.

*They're poisonous,* a smooth, echoing voice says.

My eyes grow wide. "Why would you put poisonous thorns pointing right at the entrance?" I say, stupidly talking to the bodiless voice.

*Did you expect puffy clouds and rainbows?*

I roll my eyes.

*It's a warning, foolish girl. Passing through me is equal to courting with death.*

Been there. Done that.

*Yes, you have.* The voice tsks, the voice soft and distinctly female. *A rather unpleasant turn of events.*

My eyebrows pull down. "Who are you?" I ask the vines or wall or whatever it is that's talking to me.

*Keeper of the gate,* she rumbles proudly.

"That sounds like a rough gig. How'd you get stuck with that?"

*Saving the world often requires true sacrifice. You, Caelynn of the Shadow Court, understand that well, I suspect.*

I purse my lips. I do indeed. Somehow, this being was trapped inside this wall in order to save the world? The books I read said nothing about a keeper of the gate. But it did explain the original purpose of the Schorchedlands— to keep terrible and powerful spirits inside. Is she one of those spirits trapped? Or is she doing the trapping?

*I find it no surprise the one who outwitted the Night Bringer would be so intelligent.*

I swallow. "Do you always flatter your visitors?"

*Didn't Reveln tell you of our interactions?*

I wrinkle my nose. "You could have been nicer to him."

*He shouldn't have come,* she hisses.

I sigh. "You also could have told us that!" I shake my head. "Would have been nice to know that forces of evil wanted him inside."

*They also want you inside. Will that change your mind from entering?*

I purse my lips. Touché.

*I did what I could to keep him out. It is not generally in my nature to be quite so picky about who decides to condemn themselves, but I found any and every technicality I could in this case.*

"To save him?" I ask.

*To save everyone. I was able to obey my own laws while still doing my best to safeguard my charge.*

"Your charge?"

*These cursed lands. I protect them. You and your mate are... a threat.*

"Us? You think we're going to hurt the Schorched-lands?" How would someone even do that?

*What you wish and what you will do are two very different things. You have a very interesting destiny Caelynn of the Shadow Court. I hope I'm around to watch you fulfill it. But your presence here does not bode well for my longevity.*

"Your longevity?" I ask absentmindedly, trying to work through the bits and pieces of information the being is giving me. "What do you know? What is his plan? The more information we have the more likely we can do this right."

*You have the power to do terrible things, Caelynn. With that spellbook, you will have the power to release an evil being from its rightful cage.*

"What?" I spit. "That spellbook is meant to put an end to the scourge."

*It could do that,* she agrees. *But it is not the only way to end the curse. This way was chosen for a very specific purpose that goes much beyond the scourge. There is a reason for the trials and who was entered and much more.*

I swallow. Is she saying that the Night Bringer is connected to all of it?

*You once ruined his plans,* she tells me. *It was a victorious day for the forces of good, the day Reahgan of the Luminescent Court died.*

I suck in a breath.

*I hope you will come out victorious a second time. But right now, you are following the adversary's plan quite well.*

My eyebrows pull down.

*Find the answers, Caelynn. You have allies inside these walls, but they may not be who you expect.*

I nod. Content with the information I have received. Any more and my brain might explode. I'm uncertain if I should trust an inanimate object, but nothing I've learned has changed my plans. I will go in. I will find Rev. I will make sure he gets out.

I'll deal with the rest of it as it comes.

I slice my forearm and press it on the same knob I watched Rev use.

*You wish to enter the Schorchedlands?* The feminine voice purrs, much more inhuman than just moments before.

"Yes."

*You willing submit your body to the same permanent imprisonment given to scarred souls of the dead?*

"Yes."

*Your only escape is in death, paired with redemption.*

"Death would be a mercy."

*Indeed.* Her voice sounds tired.

The vines twist and shift, slithering like snakes until a person-sized opening is laid before me.

*When your enemies are defeated, and the world safe, perhaps we can become allies in our permanent prisons.*

I suck in a breath, mind spinning to think of the years I'll spend in this place after Rev's quest is complete. Of how many this creature has already spent here.

*Good luck, Caelynn of the Shadow Court.*

I step out from her shelter and into the poisonous void before me.

It's where I always belonged. And now, I've embraced this bitter fate of mine.

# 33
## REV

The sky on the horizon lightens into a musky red. I take a swig of water and then pack up my things.

My head and heartache in sync. My muscles feel heavy and weak. But my soul is ready to complete this stupid quest and be done with it.

As a boy, I'd dreamed of being a hero, but I was never strong enough for it. One look at my perfect brother and I knew I'd never be like him. I'd never be good enough to step out from his shadow. And my father—well, he pointed out every flaw as cruelly as he could manage.

I believed, for so long, that I wasn't good enough to do anything worthwhile with my life.

But I'll prove them wrong. I'll do this.

I clench the leather straps of my backpack and march forward, through the trees, toward the south wall.

The Schorchedlands are twenty-five hundred square miles. A perfect square, which means fifty miles on each side. It's only twenty-five miles to reach the center, where the air is so thick with poisonous sulfur a living being can only survive for hours before succumbing to the death that presses in.

Which is exactly where I must travel.

But that relatively short trek is filled with spirits and obstacles that will make the trials look like a child's game.

I have a rough map of the layout, but the last person to have come through the Schorchedlands was one hundred years ago, and so much of this place is based on the magic of the spirits inside there's no telling how the terrain has changed in that time.

Once out of the copse of trees, I climb a set of average looking boulders and stop to admire the view. Well, admire is a strong word. There is nothing admirable about this place. It smells like decayed flesh, feces, and sulfur. The skyline is marred with a smog that wafts into the air so that even the sun and stars cannot be seen from this place.

I get my general bearings and pull out my compass. My path will be over the non-imposing level field of mud and muck before me. Beyond it is a shadowed forest.

There are no creatures to be seen at the moment. Everything appears simple. Easy.

I know better.

Even just my short journey last night gives me a clue that it will not be as easy of a trek as it looks. Walking only minutes brought me to a bush of thorns and mud up to my ankles. How deep will it go?

Only one way to find out.

I climb down the boulder and march into the mucky expanse. There is no water here, certainly nothing I could drink. In fact, I know that's going to be a major hurdle during my journey. There is only one place to the east that has drinkable freshwater, and it's a breeding ground for creatures looking for something new to snack on. I have to portion the water I do have and deal with the extra weight it adds. I know I can survive several days without any water at all, but I don't need a ticking timer added to my obstacles.

My boots grow heavier and heavier as I march through the mud, first sinking inches. Then, quickly, it's up to my ankles. I hope this mud doesn't have any magical properties because it's already soaking through my socks to my skin. There's nothing more I can do to get through it without using magic, which would bring attention that I don't need, and I doubt it would help much as it is.

I press on as quickly as I can manage but still sink farther and farther into the muck. Sloshing through the smelly and thick sludge, I can no longer pick my feet out entirely and just push my way through. Will I be swimming in it soon?

I grit my teeth and keep walking. My toe catches on something hard, just enough to catch me off guard. I catch my balance and keep walking.

Then, something grips my ankle. It's hard as stone, hidden beneath the thick muck at least a foot deep, clasped entirely around my ankle. I frantically shake it free and begin a high-step run. It's barely successful, but I just want to get away from whatever had me. I'd have expected a creature inside water. Not in thick mud.

But this is the Schorchedlands.

My heart pounds harder. If it gets any deeper, I may be in trouble. Before I had been comforted that if the muck pond got too deep, I could just turn around. Now, my stomach twists at the thought that I may have some kind of creature following me. I'm past it now, but that only means if I turn back I may have to face it.

My leg stings, and I lift it high enough to notice blood trickling down into my sock. *Shit.*

I grit my teeth through another scrape on my shin as I slip even deeper. Then another.

My breathing grows heavier. I'm halfway through the muck field.

High above, birds of prey have appeared, circling in the red haze above me, ready and eager for a feast.

Panic is coursing through my veins, but I can't freak out. *I can fight whatever is beneath this mud*, I tell myself.

*I hope.*

I'd so much rather have to face something massive and powerful but visible. This not knowing what's right beside me has my anxiety pulsing to the extreme. That anxiety claws at my lungs, making it hard to breathe, and messes with my head. I power through, marching as fast as I can. Something else claws at my ankle, but I quickly pull it free. It's not strong, whatever it is.

The birds screech over my head.

Then, I see something white rise from the mud out of the corner of my eye. A bone hand grasps my wrists and pulls. I yell out and rip it away only to lose my balance and tip forward. I catch myself, but my arm dips into the mud and is grabbed by several more skeleton hands.

Panic rises in my throat, and I scream. I grab my knife quickly and slash through the brittle bone.

An entire skeleton body leaps from the mud and tackles

me, arms grasping my shoulders, clamping. Muck drips over my eyes, and I scream, twisting.

"Die," it whispers in my ear.

My magic responds to my panic before I even think it through. Blinding white power explodes, sending both human bones and mud flying in all directions. I run forward as fast as I can manage, knowing I must conserve my magic but also knowing I have to do everything in my power to reach that imposing forest now just a few hundred feet away.

More skeletons rise from the mud as it settles back into place, nearly up to my waist. Bony hands grip my ankles, then my shins, then my thighs, pinning them in place. I have no choice but to use more magic or succumb to them.

They aren't strong, but they're working together now. And who knows how many there are? Thousands? Hundreds of thousands?

I send a quick blast to free my legs and keep a wall of light around me to halt any more attacks as I press on. Two hundred feet to go.

The birds sweep down toward me, and I shoot light from my palm to stop their descent. They screech as they avoid it and then continue their circle over my head, only much closer now. Anger and annoyance fill me, my terror dissipated.

*I will not fall this easily!*

My feet continue moving, plowing through the muck and continually pulling myself free from the living bones. I groan and slog through.

As the birds dive toward me a second time, I notice they are also skeletons with bits of mangled flesh hanging off their bones. I wait, pressing forward until the undead flock is only feet away, and I roar, throwing an explosion of magic at them. Several of their bodies explode into dust and sinew. A few are simply thrown back, landing into the muck and swallowed up. Three are left still flying, but they—wisely—stay back. Their high-pitched squawks send chills through me, but I continue my labored march.

One hundred feet left to go. My light barrier is staying strong, but I'm frustrated that I'll have used so much of my magic during my first obstacle. There's no telling what that forest will hold.

My energy grows thin when I finally reach the bank and—surprise, surprise—it's a steep hill covered in slippery mud. It's only about twenty feet high—just high enough I can't jump. I have to climb.

I make one attempt only to prove what I already know —climbing it will be impossible. I leap up to the slippery slope, clawing and swiping, doing my very best. And I slip right back into the waiting embrace of the bones below.

I slice through the bone with a magic lit blade until I'm freed once again.

I turn and make a second attempt at scrambling up the steep bank. There isn't anything to take a hold of. I slip right back down to their awaiting arms.

I fight my way out a second time, my breathing short and panicked. I need a plan B.

"All right," I say through ragged breaths. "Who wants to help me out?"

I turn and face the small army of bones. I'm shocked at the sheer number standing before me. I was so focused on moving forward that I didn't pay attention to their growing numbers.

They cackle at me, hissing laughter filling the air.

I'm not going to make it. It's that thought that angers me because I cannot fail. I cannot succumb this easily. *I won't!*

My anger fuels me.

It's a trick I learned from Caelynn. Shut it all out and only focus on the bad because that's what fuels your power. Passion of any kind. Love or hate. It's all the same.

Well, today I'm running on pure hatred. I don't know if it will work, but it's my last play. If I'm going to go down like this, I'll give it everything I have.

# 34
## CAELYNN

I drift in and out of restless sleep, nestled in the nook of a tree near the edge of the vine wall, and finally wake as the sun is rising over the hazy horizon. I shift, adjusting my bag full of so many random trinkets I stopped trying to keep track.

With an easy swing of my leg and a shove with my hands, I fall to the ground.

I spent some time last night looking for signs of Rev, and I quickly found some disturbance in the mud straight ahead that looked suspiciously like footprints. I followed them into a cluster of trees.

I found Rev snoozing beneath the tree in the middle of a small forest cluster. So, I made camp nearby.

The environment doesn't look much different in the morning than it had at night. Had it been just me, I'd have begun my trek immediately. But Rev doesn't see as well in the dark, and he was likely more intoxicated. Kari mentioned him taking several shots before he left.

Is Rev still sleeping, I wonder? I'm not sure what to

expect from him when he learns of my presence. Will he be angry that I followed him because he hates me now? Or will he be angry I sacrificed myself? Perhaps both.

Yes, I think both.

I slip into the shadows and sneak around to the tree he'd slept under only to find it empty. My stomach sinks. I can't lose track of him. This place is bigger than I'd expected, and I don't have the same level of instruction he does.

I know this place is square and the cure is in the center. I also know it gets more and more dangerous the closer to the center we travel. But that's about it for my knowledge. I don't even know where in the northern wall the Wicked Gate is. Do I travel straight south or do I have to curve east or west? Rev is my ticket to that information.

If I lose him, I entered this place for nothing. He'll live or die on his own.

"Come." A wispy voice drifts over the wind, curling around my head like a caress. "Look. See."

I shiver, my stomach sinking a second time. Why does that feel familiar? "Who's there?"

The voice chuckles, rumbling in the shadows between trees. I narrow my eyes. Whatever it is, their power is fairly strong.

"You don't remember me?" the voice purrs.

I put my hand on my hips and consider. There was one time in the past I had a conversation with a wraith, and it certainly felt a bit like this.

"Are you a wraith?"

Another rumble of laughter. "So, you do remember," he

purrs again and smoke shifts, forming the silhouette of a man.

It's strange to think it would be the same wraith as the one who invited me to the trials months ago. He was working for the queen of the Whisperwood at the time.

"You're no longer working for the queen?"

"Oh, no," he says as smoke drifts closer, the air around me chilling. "I still work for the queen. My job now is you."

I blink. "Me?"

"You don't think she'd just leave you to your own devices, do you?" One of the holes where its eyes should be shuts in a quick wink.

"So, what? You've been following me around?"

He smirks. "I've been watching these walls. And doing what I can to keep a certain someone from reaching you. His talons have quite a long reach, my dear. As I assume you've learned."

My mouth goes dry. "Someone?"

"I believe you know just who I speak of."

While I could come up with a few alternatives—the Luminescent Court King did send assassins for me just weeks ago—given what I've learned recently, well, it leaves me with little doubt. "I suppose I do." If he's protecting me against the Night Bringer, he's a welcomed ally—a wraith, while not exactly trustworthy is like a puppy dog compared to that monster. If he's lying, I don't intend to let him bait me any more than he already has. Let him believe me blindly faithful.

"Are you also keeping an eye on Rev, then?"

He smiles. "He is of no consequence to me." He places a

hand on his hip, and with the other, he pretends to look at his nails. Wraiths do not have nails.

"Well, you should be. I'm here for him. If you wish to keep me alive, you should protect him as well."

He chuckles. "So naive. In fact, it's exactly the opposite. That foolish prince dying, opens the gates wide for you. While he lives, you are trapped here."

I clench my jaw and smoothly pull an iron blade from its sheath at my waist. Thank you, Kari.

"Are you going to kill me?" His smile grows like he so enjoys my threat.

I widen my stance, knife held steady and my eyes locked onto the wraith before me. "If you are a threat to him, then I am a threat to you."

"Ha! Very well then. Tell me, child, if I am not a threat to him, are you an ally?"

I narrow my eyes. "Perhaps."

His smile fades into a half-grin. "Well, then, I should mention that your mate is in danger as we speak."

I stand up straight. "What?"

"He took a less than ideal route through the bog of bones. He won't survive it. No one ever has." The wraith shrugs like it's of no consequence to him.

"Where?" I yell.

He points over his shoulder past the boulder behind him. I break into action, rushing straight through the man-made of smoke and see, in the distance, a white light glowing softly surrounded by... skeletons.

"What the hell, Rev," I mutter and begin a sprint forward.

A wave of magic slams into my back and I groan, falling forward.

"I said no one has ever survived it!" the wraith spits. "That would include foolish Shadow Court females." He crosses his arms.

I stare out at the long expanse of bubbling mud. "Then, you go save him."

"Me?'" The wraith rumbles in laughter. "No. No, I am not a hero, dear. Do not mistake me."

"You want to be my ally—then, save him, you fool!" I watch in horror as Rev tries and fails to clamber up a slick wall of mud. I curse. The dead are right on him. He turns to face them.

"I already told you, if he dies, you are free to leave this place. That is in my best interest."

"You said you wouldn't be a threat to him!" Or implied it, at least.

"I will not actively take part in his death, child. But if he is so determined to put himself at risk, I will not stop it."

I grit my teeth. "Then, you'll have to watch me die trying to save him. I suppose you're used to failure." I stand and march forward.

"Wait!" the wraith calls, but I don't. I won't. I march into the muck, up to my shins in only moments. Damn, he traveled all that way in this shit? He's got to be near a mile out. I'll never make it in time without taking flight. The wraith passes in front of me. "Look! He's fighting."

"You're in the way, idiot!" I keep pushing through the mud. I won't let him die like this.

The wraith shifts so I can see Rev lit up like a freaking

star. He dims and grabs skeletons one by one and tosses them into a pile behind him.

"Come to think of it, I've never seen a fae make it that far."

"Of course, you'd say that now," I mutter, continuing my march forward.

"Stop, foolish girl. You must realize you cannot reach him. He'll either live or die by his own abilities."

"Yes, but then you wouldn't have learned an important lesson." I curl my lip. Refusing to help Rev was the wrong way to start a friendship, or whatever this creature thinks will become of us.

"What's that? You're a fool? You've made that quite clear." He shifts awkwardly. I hadn't realized wraiths had enough emotional capacity to feel nervous. I was clearly wrong.

"That Rev's life is more important than mine."

"Hush, child. You do not know what you speak of."

More skeletons leap onto Rev's back in the distance. My heart aches. *God, why wasn't I with him?* He fights his way out, light flashing here and there. The details are hard to make out, but he seems to be using the bones at his feet to climb up and over the bank. His body slowly shifts upwards, despite the bones clawing to his back.

The moment he disappears over the edge I let out a dramatic breath in relief and stop walking.

"Very good," the wraith's rumbling voice says in obvious relief. "Now, turn around, you stubborn infant."

"Stop insulting me, wraith," I yell.

"Stop acting like a child, and I will. Maybe."

# 35
## REV

My whole body aches as I fall to the flat and solid ground. The living bones still reach for me, clawing and moaning, but they don't dare push past the boundary of their sewage prison.

That was almost my fate.

What a way to spend eternity in that pit of sewage. Picked apart by savage scavengers and left to nothing but bones. I twist to face the sky, which is solid grey as if there were nothing beyond this place. No sun, no blue sky, no clouds, no future, no hope. For most of the beings here, that's true. This is their final resting place. Eternal prison.

I sit up slowly. My head throbs worse than it did this morning. I dig for a vitality potion and swallow it quickly. I used a lot of magic to escape those creatures, much more than I should have, but with a little luck, I should have enough to pass through the next obstacle. I can't afford to stop my journey for the day. After all, it's not even midday yet. There is a lot of time left in the day.

*You can do this,* I coach myself. *Be the hero your father never thought you could be.*

I don't dare consider what I will face inside the fog-filled forest staring at me. The tree trunks are a brisk white with dark patterns etched along the bark, the leaves are a dark blue. They're not terrible to look upon, which honestly scares me more. Whatever is inside won't catch me off guard this time.

I stand and attempt to brush some of the thick mud off of me, but it's caked on. What I wouldn't give for that freshwater source to clean up thoroughly. My physical energy is drained. My emotional energy is drained. But I force myself forward all the same.

I will do this because I must. Because I cannot fail.

Haunted groans drift from the rustling leaves, and I roll my eyes. "I get it, you're terrifying." I pull myself up and march into the trees.

*Reveln.* An inhuman voice tickles over my skin, and I shiver. *Reveln!* it calls again. Now, they know me. Great.

I follow the path into the forest, not daring to travel into the wild brush without guidance. There is always a way through every obstacle, as sadistic and impossible as they seem. The Schorchedlands are meant to test us in the cruelest possible way. Everything is made to trip me up, to capture me, strangle me, and make me think it's hopeless, but it will never be impossible. Which means as long as I don't let them trick me off the path, I can make it through the forest relatively unscathed.

I keep that in the back of my mind at all times. There is a path to the center of these lands, and I will find it.

When a heart gives up, that is when one surely fails. If I

believe there is a way, I will keep fighting until my last breath. It doesn't mean assured victory, because the world doesn't work that way, but it does increase my odds.

Fight, even when it feels like one no longer can.

So, I ignore the creatures calling my name. Even as they shift lower and smoother. The blue leaves rustle as I step into the shadows they cast, as if invisible forms waft through them, watching me.

The black lines etched into the trees look more and more like terror-stricken faces as I walk through the forest.

*Run,* they call to me. *Go home, Reveln.*

I swallow. The voices shift, the words, and cadence changing.

"There you are, little brother," a deep voice calls casually from inside the tree line, where the cover is thick and shadows shift.

My breath catches, but I pick up my speed and keep walking. This wouldn't be the first time I'd been tricked into thinking my dead brother was talking to me. So, I won't fall for it.

Silhouettes appear in between the trees.

Then, I hear her voice. Soft and lovely. Her golden eyes glow as she looks straight at me. "Rev," she says. "Rev, I need you."

I stop breathing entirely as my mind spins. "Caelynn?"

# 36

## CAELYNN

I slog my way back to the bank of the exceptionally smelly Bog of Bones, as the wraith called it. The mud slushes and crunches beneath me. Ew, I can't imagine walking a mile in this shit. Maybe literally.

"Where is he headed," I ask the wraith, half expecting him not to answer. He's obviously not on my side, not entirely. He wants me living, but I've been around plenty long enough to know that doesn't mean much.

The Night Bringer wanted me living. So he could torture me into doing his will. He'd have called himself an ally too. *I can give you all the things you desire.*

All you have to do is help me destroy the world and your heart along with it. No biggie.

Maybe this wraith is working for the Night Bringer.

"He'll be entering the Forest of Desires."

"That sounds better than a death bog." I roll my eyes.

"It isn't," he assures me. "The Schorchedlands are much like your trials. Each step a new challenge. Each area of the land holds a new obstacle. Only, in this game, you have no rest, no time to refuel your magic or heal your wounds. No emotional support from loved ones. This place surrounds you and quietly attacks always, even as you sleep. It will become you if you aren't careful."

I take his warnings to heart, but my mind is ready to move on. "How do I get there without passing through your death bog?"

"It isn't *my* anything," he scoffs. "I have been trying to pass on from this place for hundreds of years to no avail."

I heave in a breath. "How do I get there?" I shout. I am so not in the mood to deal with his bull shit. "Or should I go back to the damn bog and take my chances? Rev made it. I suppose I could too."

"Children," he mutters.

"I am not a child."

"Your thirty years are a fraction of my existence."

I groan. Why do I keep feeding into his foolishness? "I'm leaving," I tell him, and climb back into the muck without so much as a pause.

"Follow the edge of the bog where the stones are scattered," he finally says.

Thank you! Was that so hard?

"The distance is twice as long, but it will be a faster journey without..."

"Without waist-deep sludge and skeletons to fight off, yeah, I get it."

I don't wait to find out if there is more to his monologue. I find the stones and hop over them, sprinting when possible. The stones vary between dark charcoal and light grey, but they are easy enough to spot. I leap directly onto as many as possible but don't mind sloshing into the muck of the bog when it's an easier path. I simply don't stay long.

My feet are already caked with mud and those skeletons aren't nearby—yet.

He's right; this path is much easier. I may not have noticed the stones marking the edge of the bog without his instructions. They travel out and around in an oval, nearly doubling the distance, but my feet are free to travel at a quick speed, and I use that to my advantage. These two miles take several minutes before I find the bank slope still clearly marked with Rev's and the skeleton's claw marks.

I purse my lips and take a good long look around.

"Do you still require my help to find your prince charming, my lady?"

I roll my eyes because there is a very clear and obvious path of mud dripping from the bank of the bog into the trees.

"Don't call him that. And don't call me a lady," I say, beginning my trek onto the pathway.

"Ahh, yes, I recall your disgust with your title. Why is that, do you suppose?"

"I am not a countess any more. I was stripped of my title many years ago."

"And you still blame yourself for your crime."

"I am not sorry for killing Reahgan. But it was murder nonetheless, and I deserve the punishment."

"Was it truly murder?" the wraith says in a sing-song voice. His smoke dissolves and drifts right over me. I shiver but continue my march, eyes examining the trees as we walk.

He forms in front of me, but I do not falter and walk

right through him again. Leave it to me to get the most annoying tagalong ever. Who even gains a damn side-kick inside hell?

"Because I heard you were simply defending yourself." He sounds so damned pleased with himself.

"Do not talk about things you do not know," I spit, repeating his own words. Yes, Reahgan was an ass. Yes, he was the kind of fae to enjoy hurting someone else. Yes, he would have hurt me if I hadn't fought back. But one doesn't feel the kind of pleasure I got the moment Reahgan's life left him unless they're bad to the very core.

"I know quite a bit more than you think, my dear."

"What is your intention, wraith?" I stop hands on my hips. "In helping me."

"What's in it for me, you mean?"

"I don't much care what a wraith wants. No. Whose will are you completing? Who do you work for?"

His smoky lips curl into a grin. "I am working directly for the Shadow Court Queen."

I narrow my eyes but continue walking down the dirt path through the forest. "What does she intend to achieve by helping me?" There is an obvious answer, but I still question it.

"Isn't it obvious?" he slurs his words. "She wants you to be her successor. You, my dear, are the strongest shadow fae in centuries. With you, our court has a chance at reestablishing our lost heritage. With you, we can rebuild."

"We," I repeat.

"I was once a Shadow Court king, did you not know that?"

My eyebrows pull down. He'd claimed the Shadow

Court as his own before, but king?

*Don't let him distract you*, I remind myself. His story, his history, is of no consequence. He may not even be telling the truth. *Do not trust a wraith.*

"Right."

"She did not want to stick her hand too deeply into the trials for fear of disqualifying you. But she's been hoping you'd come to see her in the Shadow Court. She's been waiting for you."

My heart aches. I don't trust the wraith, but I do love my court. And I had wished to visit. I'd wanted to give them a boost of my power. What little I could give for the temporary time I'd been allowed to stay. But I never made it.

"I planned to do just that. It just... didn't happen."

"Your mate lured you into his clutches. I know. It's happened many times to many promising young ladies. It's how they continued to weaken us, you know? My own child was forced into marriage in the Flicker Court."

My eyebrows rise at his confession.

It's well known that shadow fae have been forced to join other courts. Sometimes male, but often it's the strongest females of the Shadow Court that are targeted. My own parents discussed the possibility of sending me away as an adolescent.

After generations, it left us with only weak pairings and, therefore, weaker children. Our magic slowly siphoned out of our lands.

"I didn't fall into his clutches. There's no hope for Rev and me," I say, my voice hollow. "But he needed my help. And I couldn't abandon him."

"In the same way, you couldn't leave him to his own devices on his own quest? You sacrificed yourself—again. Was that always your plan?"

"No," I whisper. Shadows shift past the trees as we pass them. I narrow my eyes. "What was that?"

"Nothing of consequence," the wraith says, drifting around me. "Why did you come here then, child? Was your life so terrible you decided to end it early? You obviously have no sense of value for your own life."

"No," I say again. I blink and turn to watch my boots stomping on the uneven path. We are moving rather slowly. "Once I learned the Night Bringer was setting a trap for Rev..."

The wraith cackle laughs. "That's what you heard? From what source?"

I purse my lips. Again, another shift in the forest outside the pathway.

"He's been setting a trap for *you*."

I stop and cross my arms. "I realize he also wants me here. I don't know why, nor do I care."

"Oh my." His voice is quiet, less amused than his words would imply. "I expected more from the child who outwitted the Night Bringer."

I stop and roll my eyes, the wraith once again blocking my path.

"Your Night Bringer cannot even enter these lands without becoming trapped. He is not here."

I narrow my eyes. How had I not considered that? His shifts oddly, waving his hands as if trying to keep my attention.

"Don't worry, your conclusions are not far off. It's

simply the dismissal of your own life that is wrong. For the Night Bringer is not the only ancient being you should fear, Caelynn of the Shadow Court."

My eyes flick beyond the wraith to someone standing in the path before us. The wraith's smoke body shifts to block the view. "There is someone inside these walls just as evil as the monster that haunts your dreams."

"You're distracting me," I say.

His nose wrinkles.

I sidestep him to see a lovely black haired fae with a crown of swirling black magic on her head. My eyebrows pull down. The queen of the Whisperwood is here?

The wraith leaps back in front of me. "All for your own good, child."

"What is this place?" I ask finally. We've walked half a mile without me noticing much of anything. Now that I've stopped to pay attention, the leaves above rustle with movement. They shift and pull, crunching beneath the feet of creatures unseen.

My breath comes quicker.

"The forest of desires," he says, and I do recall him using that name once already. "Distraction is the best form of defense against this place."

"It shows you the things you desire?" I ask, eyes casting around me.

"It deceives you. The creatures create illusions of your deepest desires to lure you in. Creatures who will devour you, body, and soul. They'll hypnotize you into believing them."

"And if you give in," I start, and the queen in the trees just off the path takes off her crown and holds it out to me.

That wouldn't be such a bad way to die, would it? "If you get too close…"

"They will eat you alive. And you'll thank them for it."

I blink, remembering something important. "Where's Rev?"

"Why should I know? Oh! Better question—why should I *care?*"

I groan and turn back.

"Rev!" I call. I sprint down the path of this simple forest of white trees, scanning the shadows for any sign of Rev. I stop when I see a couple dancing. She wears a masquerade mask and a black dress adorned with glistening crystals. He wears a clean black suit with a white tie and smile that makes my heart melt.

That was the day I met Rev.

That was the day I was ordered to kill him.

I step closer to the spinning couple, eyes pinned to them. The girl disappears and the boy—Rev of ten years ago, Rev whose brother is still alive, Rev who doesn't know who I am, what I am—turns to me. His eyes are bright silver, innocent, happy. He holds his hand out to me.

Me. Real me.

Rev wants me.

I blink, heart aching.

"Caelynn!" the wraith calls to me. "It isn't real."

"I know," I whisper, blinking again. "I was just thinking… Perhaps when this is all over and I've ensured Rev is safe and out of this place, his quest fulfilled, that I'd come back here. And I'd dance with him one more time, before—"

"NO!" the wraith growls, grabbing my arms. His grip

cannot hold me, the smoke dissolves over me, but his magic sears shooting pain through my whole body. A wraith can't physically move a living being, but it can certainly hurt one. It can easily kill me if it desires.

"Ow!" I yell, pulling away from him and rubbing the red patches of skin where he touched me. "That burned."

"Look," he tells me, pointing toward a tree trunk carved into the shape of arms reaching out. No, not carved. It is a person. His eyes are hollow, lifeless, his mouth open in a silent scream, begging. His fingers are curled, eager to grasp me.

"You turn in to that if you succumb to those desires."

I swallow.

"This is where most soul's journey ends. Stuck here where their desires are at their fingertips but never within reach."

"Sounds like my life."

"These creatures feed off your desperate desires, not your happiness. You'll live a half-life. Stuck here with your own pain relived over and over again."

I swallow. Okay, less pleasant than I'd imagined.

"There is no escape for these souls. No hope of passing on."

I take in a long breath. "Where is Rev?" I ask again. "The real one."

The wraith nods behind me to a form standing in the middle of the path. His mud-covered clothes are ripped and bloodied. *What happened to him?*

Next to him stands a blond female—me.

# 37
## REV

Caelynn stands before me, her eyes are so soft and gentle. She licks her lips and looks down at mine.

*Not real*, I tell myself. *Not real.*

I was warned about this forest; although, I hadn't realized what I was walking into until the mirages started happening. My brother and I playing tag in the iridescent forest. The High Queen offering me her crown. My father kneeling before me.

And Caelynn. First, she sat laughing and talking with Reahgan as friends. An accepted part of my family.

That wasn't something I'd ever even bothered to picture, but damn if it wasn't the most beautiful sight. And therefore, the most painful.

This place is a slide show of all the things I'll never have.

Then, Caelynn stepped toward me, slowly, deliberately. Lovely, young, unscarred, in a smooth white silk dress, beckoning to me. Her eyes are bright gold, and she runs her tongue over her plump bottom lip. I swallow.

*Not real. Not real.*

I can't help but feel desire deep in my gut. The strap of her silky dress slips down her shoulder, and my mouth goes dry.

I take one small step toward her, my toe just hanging off the edge of the path. That's when the trees reach for me. Their claws sharp as iron, slice into my arm before I pull away. Caelynn begins begging for my help, swallowed up in the vicious limbs.

My iron blade is out in an instant, and I desperately slash at the branches, trying to hook me like a damn fish. I cut through the branches surrounding me, trip back onto the dirt path, and scramble backward too far. My hand drops onto the grass—off the pathway.

An arm clasps me from behind, soft at first. She whispers in my ear, "I want you, Rev."

Then, her fingers dig into my chest, breaking the skin and dragging me back into the forest.

Suddenly, someone grabs my shoulder and throws me back into the dirt, the only safe place from the clawing trees and evil spirits, apparently.

The silky-dressed Caelynn stands right at the edge of the forest, her eyes just as soft and full of desire as before. I turn away from that Caelynn and toward—another one.

*What the hell?*

"It's not real, Rev!" she shouts at me.

"You think I don't know that?"

The silk-dressed Caelynn hisses at the other. I slice my

iron blade through her chest and she shrivels away into dust.

The other Caelynn on the open pathway, where the trees cannot reach, is disheveled, her hair pinned awkwardly almost like it had been for the Queen's gala except half fallen out. She wears new clothes—a leather ensemble I've never seen. Her boots are caked with mud. And a wraith stands behind her.

She steps back, her eyes dark and full of fear. This doesn't seem like a mirage of desire. This feels... real.

I open my mouth, but nothing comes out. My iron blade shakes in my hand.

Caelynn holds up her hands. "I'm not here to hurt you. I'm real."

"No," I whisper. "No, you can't be real. You have to be... something. Some kind of trick." But something deep in my gut tells me not to hurt this Caelynn. My breathing comes faster, racing as if to keep up with my galloping heart. "You wouldn't be here. Couldn't," I ramble on.

She reaches for me, and I stumble away, refusing to face—whatever this is. I have to get away from her. From the truth. Because if Caelynn is here... it means something is very wrong. It means everything is wrong.

I stumble and step off the path and into the awaiting claws.

# 38
## CAELYNN

"No! Rev!" I call after him, and he stumbles into the tree cover. They pull him in, swallowing him whole. "NO!"

"Don't you dare— "my babysitter wraith cries just as I flee into the forest after him. The trees reach for me, white, mummy-like appendages with talon-like fingers.

I swipe viciously at the newly formed wall of tree limbs and vines until I'm able to burst through to the open forest.

Just feet ahead Rev is imprisoned by a tree with four human-like arms over his own arms and chest. He thrashes, but he's unable to get free. Another tree grabs at me, but my anger rises.

*They will not take him from me.* That's all I can think, all I can feel—rage.

My shadow power blasts from my body, splintering the branches nearest to me. Then, I send a blast at the tree holding Rev.

Suddenly free, Rev drops onto the ground with a crunch, and his hands come up slick with blood. Gory body parts I hadn't noticed before litter the ground everywhere. *God, this place is a nightmare.*

"Run!" I yell to Rev.

He scrambles up and slams his shoulder through the blockage of arm-like branches. He stumbles, tripped by white vines crawling from under the blood-soaked ground. I blast through the demons who would dare touch my mate with a simple thought. My mind is on fire. Rage and panic covering every coherent thought.

I stumble forward, watching as Rev reaches the safety of the pathway and falls to his knees, breathing deeply.

Then, several branches clasp onto my upper body at once. The vines shoot from the ground and wrap tightly around my legs. I struggle, but I can't move.

I'm pulled to the largest tree, my back pressed tightly against it, my chest so constricted I can't breathe. A hand presses into my back, sharp claws dig into my skin, and I scream in agony. My vision goes black as pain fills my thoughts.

*No*, I think, *not again. Not this.*

Instead of good memories, instead of desire, I remember him.

His talon searing into my stomach, severing my soul from my body. A sob wracks my body, tears streaming as the memories of the Night Bringer tearing my soul apart bombard me.

Then, my vision goes entirely black.

# 39
## REV

I watch in horror as the disheveled Caelynn is swallowed by the very tree that tried to take me. I can't figure out what's real and what's not.

She seems so real. And if... if this place is the forest of desires, meant to tempt you with all the things you want most in order to lure you to your death—why would it be showing her dying? Why would her agonized screams be so life-like?

And why would she have helped me escape?

Is it a trick? If I try to help her...

The wraith I'd seen earlier barrels into the forest toward her, its echoing screams rumbling, shaking the ground. He blasts magic into the tree, and Caelynn's body drops like a rock.

"Shit!" he groans, fighting with more vines that have already begun wrapping around her fallen body. She's unconscious. "Help me!" the wraith calls. "I can't move her!"

I cannot figure this out. Why would Caelynn be here?

And why would a wraith care about her death?

I shake my head and make a snap decision. I go with my gut, and I rush into the deadly forest to help someone who very well may be a demon in disguise.

At best, it's a fae who ripped my heart to shreds. Who I'm supposed to hate. But what I'm supposed to feel and what I really feel are nowhere near the same.

The wraith blasts away the vines covering her, and I grab her limp body, groaning with the effort it takes to throw her over my shoulder.

She's bleeding from a wound in her back. It drips down my shoulder, warming me. My stomach turns, leaving me nauseous.

The wraith continues throwing his magic at the trees surrounding us, carving out a pathway for me to reach the opening.

I drop Caelynn's limp body onto the ground and gasp in breaths. "What the hell?"

"Don't just leave her there, foolish lumi. Pick her up."

"You're rather demanding."

"You nearly got her killed and ruined my chances of freedom, so pardon me if I'm not all roses and sunshine at the moment."

"Isn't she already doomed just by being here?" I say under my breath. My stomach sinks as that reality sinks in. I stare at the soft lines of her face.

Caelynn is really here. And she's never going to leave.

"Indeed. But there is hope yet, princeling."

I roll my eyes but gently lift Caelynn into my arms. One arm cradling her head and another under her legs.

"That's right, come on, kid."

"If you're going to chat incessantly, you might as well tell me what the hell is happening? Why is she here? Is she even real? And why are you helping us?"

"Her. I am helping her; there is no us as far as I'm concerned."

I narrow my eyes. Don't trust the wraith. Got it. Not that I'd intended to trust him.

"However, to my displeasure, I require your assistance. So, consider yourself on my team. For now." He continues grumbling about the stupidity of living folk.

I'm already exhausted from my trip through the swamp and the forest, so carrying a dead weight fae—even one as slight as Caelynn—is not particularly easy. I walk slowly through the forest with some random wraith grumbling pathetically in my wake.

I am careful with each step, knowing any moment I step off the narrow pathway, I am within reach of the trees—or whatever they actually are. Those white-barked trees are exponentially creepier now that I've seen what they can do, how their hands claw at you like human limbs. I shiver.

In the shadows between the trees, there is a slideshow of memories. I blink and turn away as my attention catches on an entirely naked Caelynn standing right at the edge of the forest.

I swallow, face burning.

Yes, I want to know what she looks like beneath her clothes. No, it's not a good idea to indulge such unhealthy thoughts. She is my enemy. She's always been my enemy; she just did a hell of a good job hiding that for a while.

Part of me thinks I should just drop her here in the

middle of this trail and leave her behind. But I have entirely too many questions. And well... as angry as I am with her— as much as I don't trust her—she has helped me in the past. I shake my head. I have no idea what to think about her anymore.

"This is not how I expected my time in the Schorched-lands to go," I mutter.

"It never is," the wraith sighs.

I focus on each step, ignoring the illusions tempting me from within the trees.

My father, my real father watches me with admiration. Pride. I don't even know what my real father looks like. I hadn't cared enough to find out. But somehow, I know the man between the white trees is my biological father.

And his eyes tell me he's proud of me. I shiver and force myself to keep walking.

Having Caelynn in my arms, and the distraction of all of those questions stirring around in my mind has made it easier to ignore the temptations.

I am certainly going to have nightmares about the Schorchedlands for the rest of my life. There are stories about fae who spent months and even years in this place.

How? How is it even possible to have survived that long?

Finally, I see an opening up ahead. Only a few hundred more feet to go. What horror will face me when I complete this terrible task? It's only going to get worse, according to legend. "Okay," I say finally. "Tell me what is happening, will you?"

The wraith groans and throws his smoky hands in the air in exasperation. "I am to keep this stupid, foolish, idiotic female alive. And first, she runs off into the Schorchedlands—where, surprise, she cannot ever return from. Then, she nearly throws herself into the bog to go after you, and then she *does* succeed in throwing herself into the Forest of Desires to go after you. What's a wraith to do? I can't work with this. You'd think she was human, the way she throws her life around like it doesn't matter!"

I was only half-listening as he went on and on about Caelynn's irrational acts. All of them following me. Why? What is she doing here?

If this is really Caelynn—and more and more I'm beginning to believe it is truly her and not some trick of the Schorchedlands—she has doomed herself. Only one can enter and return.

Caelynn will never leave this place alive.

"Why?" I say softly. "Why did she come here?"

"You will be the death of her, boy."

I roll my eyes. "I am not a boy."

"May as well be."

"Why?" I ask again.

"Because she's foolhardy and noble and quick to act. She feels duty-bound to kill herself to save her mate when he's in mortal danger."

"It's the Schorchedlands. Of course, I'm in danger. That's the point."

The wraith chuckles darkly. "Indeed. However, she's unfortunately uncovered there is more to the plot. And even though she knew coming here would make it worse, she came anyway to save the life of her beloved mate. Who is idiotic enough to hate her."

I clench my jaw. My first inclination is to deny it. I look

down at her limp body in my arms, her head bobbing awkwardly.

*I do hate her*, I remind myself. She's... evil. Bad to the core. She belongs here.

I try to force the thoughts to be true. Like my mind could override my heart.

It's only the magic of the mating bond. It wants me to love her. It's not real. None of it was ever real. I clench my jaw at the wave of pain that floods me.

My breathing picks up speed. I should drop her on the ground here and now and leave her behind. Leave her to her strange wraith friend in the place she clearly belongs. I could move ahead and ensure she isn't around to continue screwing with my head.

The wraith grunts and groans dramatically as he floats along beside me.

Who else would befriend the soul of an evil fae but her? There is a reason he took this form after his death—because deep down he was evil. Just like she is.

Maybe she realized it too. She's at home with creatures like this wraith.

*A damn wraith!* I shake my head. *Following after her like a puppy.*

"Why should she bother to save someone who hates her?" The wraith continues to complain. "Why worry about a relationship that was doomed from the start? She continues sacrificing for you. Over and over. She chose you over meeting with her queen. Then, she uncovered the secret to the Wicked Gates and broke her own heart to help you. It's pathetic."

"What secret?" I ask suddenly. "The secret to the Wicked Gate?"

"You're so stupid you still haven't figured it out." The wraith sighs. "Let me ask you a riddle, child. Perhaps, one day, you'll figure it out, and you'll know what really happened."

I sigh. *A riddle, perfect.*

"What is the quest every soul takes up when they enter the Schorchedlands?"

My eyebrows furrow. "Find redemption."

"Indeed."

I blink. "That's it? That's the riddle?" It didn't give me any more answers.

"That's it. Figure out how it pertains to you, and perhaps you'll see what is right before your eyes."

I bite the inside of my lip.

"What is this plot?" I ask, looking to change the subject. This is the more important subject anyway. She came here for a reason, and the wraith implied some grand scheme. "My father sent assassins after me?"

"Very funny, child. This is much bigger than your pompous father and your family issues."

"Then, what?"

"You've had a target on your head since you were a child. You both have. Deep within the lowest and darkest places, where the worst of the worst dwell, there have been rumblings about you and your mate for many years."

I swallow. "Why?" I ask blandly. I don't know how much I buy into anything he says at this point, but I might as well hear the whole story.

"Isn't that the question?" He shakes his head. "You

each have an ability that either side of an ancient war would like to use. Those powerful beings of darkness wish you dead to stop you from learning to wield this power. And her." The wraith sighs. "She has the ability to do many good things but also terrible. She has the right blood and now, the power to complete the task."

"What task?" It's so vague it's driving me insane.

"She has the magic needed to unite them. She can free a terrible ancient being that has been trapped in the Schorchedlands for a thousand years. It's ironic that she has always desired freedom above all else—even above you, boy—and that is exactly what those creatures desire too."

"That's it? They desire freedom?"

The wraith chuckles. "No, they desire much more. That is simply the first step. There is a reason she was contained in the first place, child. If the Night Terror is reunited with her mate... They would commit acts that make the scourge look like a child's attempt at vengeance. They will desolate the whole realm as easy as blinking."

"So, if Caelynn has this power, her death would end it all. Would it not?"

"It would. However, that is not my goal. I wish to free Caelynn from her banishment—and now, this place—so that she can breathe life back into my court."

"You wish to revive the Shadow Court to its former glory." I clench my jaw through the searing pain in my back.

"Indeed. And I do not wish for those evil beings to be freed because if they are, there will be no more Shadow Court. There will be no more courts at all."

# 40
## CAELYNN

I groan and roll onto my stomach. Stabbing pain shoots through my back, and several images flash through my mind. Rev, the wraith, the thorn wall of the Schorchedlands, trees with flesh-like arms trying to devour me.

I force my eyes open and cough. There's pressure on every part of my body. Every muscle clenching.

Heaving in a heavy breath, I look around. A small fire flickers in the darkness, a large stone shelters one side of the small camp against the wind, which howls around us. I blink, finding Rev sitting on the other side of the fire wide awake.

"Rev?" I croak.

"There's a potion beside you. Take it; it'll help."

I wince but reach for a small vial of red potion. I toss it back quickly. It burns, and I wince again but quickly my limbs feel steadier, the pain receding slightly. I force my body to sit up.

"Ahh! Sleeping Beauty awakens," a rumbling voice calls

and a smoky silhouette forms before me.

I groan again. "What the hell happened?"

"You, once again," the wraith purrs, "tried to off yourself to save that fool. Stop doing that, will you?" He says it like I'm a child in class. I never did like teachers.

"How in the world did you end up in league with a wraith?" Rev says with a low and annoyed voice.

"I'm not so sure myself."

The wraith grunts. "Go to sleep, children. We'll have a long day tomorrow."

I narrow my eyes and watch as he drifts off over the stone and disappears. I don't know what to make of him. He wants me living, but it sounds as though he's intending to help us complete Rev's quest now. Or will he turn on us?

My eyes meet Rev's beyond the fire. Every line of his face is harsh, his eyes angry. Despite the hate radiating off of him now—talk about déjà vu—he helped me. We're no longer in that forest, which means he must have carried me out of it, set up camp, including the sleeping bag under me and the flickering fire between us. The wraith could not have done any of that.

"What are you doing here, Caelynn?"

I wince at Rev's harsh tone and look down at my lap. "I'm surprised you went to so much effort to save me," I say, changing the subject and brushing down the folds in my sleeping blanket.

"I shouldn't have, and I don't suspect I will again." He pauses. "But I needed to know. Why in the realm would you enter through those gates knowing you'll never return?" There is no sadness in his voice or expression as he says the words. It doesn't bother him that I have a new prison in this evil place. He probably thinks I belong here.

He's not entirely wrong.

"After what you said to me—" His lip curls into almost a snarl like he'd love nothing more than to bite my head off. "How you'd have the nerve to face me again is beyond me. What could be so important that you'd doom yourself to come here? Do you wish to kill me and take the glory for yourself?"

I bark out a bitter laugh. "You think that little of me, do you?" I continue a dark chuckle. I'm not entirely surprised but can't deny a bit of disappointment. He didn't see through my lies at all. He's more than hurt and angry. He believed it entirely.

It was so easy to push him away.

I sniff, pushing the wave of sorrow back down to the depths of my shattered soul. "And how do you explain me saving you inside the forest of desires? How does that fit into your narrative?"

He grunts.

"Your father has made a deal with the Night Bringer." I shrug. "They both want you dead. There's something here they want. Something *he* wants. And they need me to get it. The plan was to kill you within these walls, and then I would be next in line to enter."

"So, they want you here and your idea is... to come anyway?"

"It was that or leave you to death. I assume we'll both have a better chance if we work together."

"We are not partners, shadow fae. We are not allies. We will not be working together."

I bit the inside of my lip, frustration filling to overflowing. "Then, leave me behind," I say low and slow. "And when you get into trouble, I'll be there to pull you out. Then, you'll be free to continue hating me. It's a vicious cycle. But I suppose it's what we're best at."

I'm good at pushing people away. Rev is good at anger and lying to himself.

# 41

## REV

I should sleep, but my mind rebels against even the thought. I twist and turn, muscles aching, and mind whirling.

*Caelynn is here.*

That thought sends a sharp ache through my heart. She's here, and she'll never leave.

As much as I try to convince myself that I hate her, I know it isn't true. Not entirely. I'm so angry with her, and I can't see through the rage sometimes. And then, other times, I'm hypnotized by her strength, her bravery, and selflessness. I'm lost in the way she looks at me.

It kills me to think I'll have to leave her here. This hellish place that will fill my nightmares for life. She'll be living it. Forever.

She'll never escape this evil place. Because of me.

She came to protect *me*.

I shake my head, trying to figure her out. No matter what kind of scum lies over her heart, she loves me—I think that much I can justify. Her heart and soul are so smothered in pain and trauma it's consumed her.

*I loved it*, she said about killing my brother. I press my eyes closed tightly as a fresh wave of pain hits me. It wouldn't hurt this bad if...

It shouldn't hurt this bad.

*I'd do it again if given the chance, and I'd enjoy it just as much.*

It's hard to breathe as daggers press through my chest. I can feel it, the place she stabbed him. Where she carved a hole in his chest and mine in the same moment.

Hating her is easy. It's what I've been doing since I was barely an adult. And so, I fall back to it, even while knowing I cannot commit entirely.

She's stolen my heart, and that's the crime I can never forgive.

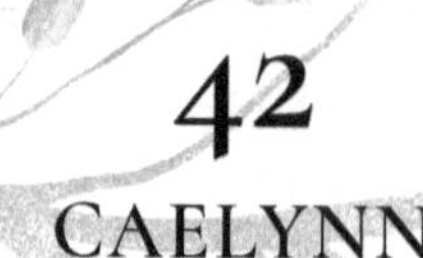

# 42
## CAELYNN

R ev is sleeping when I wake. My body still aches terribly, and my back roars with pain, like a thousand razor blades embedded into my skin that bite every time I shift even slightly.

I press my hand against the wound, and my hand comes away slick with black blood. That's probably not good. What kind of poison do these creatures have in their fangs and claws?

I pull in a few long breaths and then force myself to stand with wobbly knees. I might be screwed. Rev doesn't trust me—not that I blame him. And I'm here with no other allies than this tagalong wraith. And I'm injured. Maybe gravely injured.

I lift my shirt and tie a quick bandage over the wound.

"About time you woke."

I spin to find the wraith dancing over the fire. A hole where his mouth would be opens into an oddly curled smile.

It's not pleasant.

The sky is only just beginning to lighten, so it's not as if we slept in. I ignore the wraith and make an achingly slow climb over the stones we were sheltered by, and I find a good vantage point. Down below us is a massive valley of red stone several miles wide beneath a huge set of mountains. A grey stone valley peppered with hundreds, maybe thousands, of wraiths.

"Whoa," I mutter. "Is this Death Valley?"

The wraith nods. "These are the mindless wraiths," he tells me. "Two-thirds of the souls who are sent to the Schorchedlands are caught in either of the first two obstacles. They become bones in the Bog of the Dead, or they are trapped by the trees in the Forest of Desires. The ones who escape those common fates are free to travel throughout the lands. But there is little for us to live for. And so, after many years, many lose their hope and, finally, their minds. Those wraiths wander this barren valley for eternity." His voice is so much more somber than before, and I wonder if he knows some of the wraiths wandering below personally. I wonder if he expects he'll join them one day.

I swallow, watching the ghost-like wraiths. They waft in the gentle wind, passing back and forth, back and forth.

"We have to pass through them?"

"Yes," he says, "The wraiths hide while the sun is up. Many have already scattered. You do not want to be caught in the valley at night. As mindless as those spirits are, they will not hesitate to kill a living being that crosses their path. At night there will be so many you cannot walk a foot without stumbling into one."

I nod, accepting his advice. "Do you know where to find the spellbook?" I ask, not expecting an answer. Even if he did know, why would he help? He doesn't want Rev to complete his mission.

"Pass between those two mountains. There will be another few obstacles before you reach the acid swamp. The book is there. In the center of it all."

Acid swamp. That sounds *lovely*.

"What are you discussing?"

I whip around, the fast movement sending jolts of pain through my body. Through my blurred vision, I find Rev standing at the bottom of the largest stone, looking up at us.

"Just what lies between us and the spellbook."

He climbs up to the top of the stone. "Which is?" His jaw is tight and eyes cast over the field below.

"A field populated by wraiths. Only passable in the sunlight, apparently."

"Even in the sunlight, it isn't easy. There will be lingering wraiths. Luckily, you have me." The wraith does his creepy smoke smile again.

"I would never align with a wraith." Rev's lip curls in disgust. "If you think I'm going to let you take this from me and leave me behind..."

The wraith burst out laughing. "Is that what you think she's doing? Trying to usurp you? Well, I wish. Indeed, that would make my life much easier."

"Whatever," Rev says and turns to pack up his things.

I sigh, willing to allow Rev to have his tantrum—I don't blame him for his distrust or his hate, but the wraith leaps after him.

"And what is wrong with wraiths?" he asks, curling around him. "You think yourself so morally superior?"

"Wraith are evil souls. Of course, I'm more moral."

"You are such an oblivious fae. One day, the truth you work so hard to fight will smack you in the face, and you'll realize how wrong you've been."

"You're so damn cryptic." Rev shakes his head. "Good thing I don't care what you mean."

"What do you think was the reason you couldn't enter through the gates before? What changed that allowed you entry? Let me give you a hint. It was your soul. You didn't belong here, Prince Reveln. The gate tried everything it could to keep you out for all our sakes."

"What the hell are you talking about?"

"Wraith," I warn. Rev does not need to know all of this.

"And," the wraith goes on, "what if it turned out you knew one of those wraiths down there? Would you still act so superior?"

Rev jerks back. "No one I've known would have come to this place."

"Ha!" the wraith spits, spinning in the air like he enjoys this. "How about Rook, your friend that betrayed you? That your mate you hate so much killed to protect you? The fae guard who attempted to kill a teenaged human just to get to your lovely mate? Or how about Reahgan?"

Before I can even blink, white light blasts from Rev's palm, slamming into the wraith. He screams in agony as the light presses him into the ground. The smoke that makes up his wraith body convulses.

"Rev!" I call, but he doesn't hear me. He doesn't register anything in his blinding rage.

I toss a wall of shadow magic between them, cutting off the searing white light. Rev doesn't seem to care—he got his point across. "Don't you dare talk about my brother."

Rev grabs his bag and stomps away, toward the valley filled with wraiths below.

# 43
## REV

My wraith groans. "Charming lover of yours."

"He's not my lover. And I didn't choose him, magic chose him for me."

He chuckles bitterly. "If you could sever the mating bond, would you do it?"

I jerk away from him, stomach in my mouth. "What the hell are you talking about?"

"I didn't think so."

Is such a thing possible? And even if it were possible, why would I? To save myself some pain? No, I have grown quite accustomed to pain.

"Just because the magic makes *its* choice known, doesn't mean your choice isn't also part of the equation. You do not have to love your fated mate."

I bite the inside of my lip, shove my remaining things into my bag, and stomp out the last of the embers of our flame.

"He is going to get himself killed storming out there like that," the wraith tells me.

I sigh and begin a slow trek down the hillside toward the open field. "The ground isn't going to swallow him whole here, is it?"

"No. But that doesn't mean it's any safer."

Rev's silhouette is visible in the distance, but so long as I can see him, that's okay with me. This valley is so flat and open I can see for miles.

The faded glow of sunlight is just now lightening the sky and already the valley is mostly clear of its wraith inhabitants. There are several still slinking to the tree line on both sides and two or three visible wraiths wafting in the shadows below the mountains, but none anywhere nearby. Even so, I pull shadows around my body so I'm less noticeable.

"You see," my wraith says, "smart. Unlike that fool."

I roll my eyes and continue my march, keeping a close eye on the shifting shadows far in the distance. They dance at every edge of this place.

I ache to catch up to Rev, but I know better. He needs some space, and I could probably use it too. The truth is, being near him is hard. Looking him in the eyes and knowing the male I love hates me, for good reason, and I will never have the opportunity to change his mind—hurts really bad.

So, I keep my distance and just watch. If he needs my help, I'll leap in. If he doesn't, I'll leave him to wallow in his own delusions.

Rev is nearly halfway to the mountain range when something massive shifts up ahead, over a hundred yards off our trajectory but close enough that my stomach sinks. "Oh shit," the wraith says.

I stop, breath caught in my throat. A roaring beast, at least triple the size of a bear but with a distinctively similar gait, charges forward.

Straight toward Rev.

# 44
## REV

My eyes grow wide as a huge beastly creature roars, charging straight at me.

The pathway was so open, wide, and clear, I thought... *shit*. Obviously, I thought wrong.

A bear made of bone and rotting flesh, at least thirty feet tall charges straight at me. I'm alone with nowhere to hide.

I slide my sharp obsidian sword out of its sheath, gripping it tightly in one hand and my iron dagger in the other. I widen my stance ready to take on the monster. My light magic will draw a lot of attention to me, and here in the middle of an open plain miles long, with wraiths lining the edges, is a really bad place to attract attention.

This fight is going to have to be magicless.

I said I'd rather take on an impossible opponent face to face than creatures clawing at me from where I can't see them.

Well, I meant it.

And when the bear reaches me, teeth bared and dripping with green slime, I spin and slice in one fluid motion. The beast roars, more in anger than pain, and whips around much faster than I'd anticipated, and his talon clips my thigh, slicing through the skin.

I leap to my feet, ignoring the raging pain in my leg and the trickle of warm blood seeping through my pants. There will be time to heal it later.

The monster bear stops a dozen feet from me, heaving in breaths and snorting. But he doesn't move. He just watches me with black pits where there should be eyes.

He lifts his chin, strings of bloody flesh hanging off awkwardly. I suppress a gag and then sprint straight at him. He returns the gesture and runs for me, his roar echoing over the open field, reverberating off the mountains in the distance.

The moment I'm within range of his mangy paws, I fall to my hip and slide beneath him. I shove up with the iron blade through bone and pieces of flesh. But before I carve his heart, he twists, his massive boney paw slamming down, and I roll out of the way just before he crushes me.

My arm is covered in oozing flesh tinged with green and red, but the beast is still quite lively.

Another shadow comes into focus, pulling my attention from the bear for just a moment, and that instant of distraction costs me. He lands another swipe with his razor-sharp claws—right over my torso.

I scream body tossed to the ground. My vision turns black for only a moment, then I leap back to my feet. Caelynn is beneath the beast, carving at his leg. She manages to remove a large piece of bone before he reaches her with his powerful jaws.

For a moment, I'm angry with her. Can't she just leave me be? Doesn't she believe I'm strong enough to do this on my own?

But then, her body is swept up into the monster's massive mouth. She screams, and panic fills my every limb.

*No.*

Without even thinking, a blast of white-hot power explodes from my palm toward the beast. Caelynn's limp body falls to the ground with a crunch. The bear whines, high pitched and pathetic, clawing at his eyes.

Curling my hands into a circle, I build a sphere of magic. "Move," I yell at Caelynn, praying she's able. Secretly begging her to be okay.

She cries out but manages to roll her body over and again. It'll have to do.

I leap toward the bear, hands pressed to his chest, and just before his claws tear me to shreds, I detonate my magical sphere.

The undead-bear flies fifty feet into the air and lands with a crash that rumbles the ground beneath me.

Birds leap from the trees at least a mile east and flock towards us.

Great. So much for not drawing attention.

At least the bear's body is crumpled in an unmoving heap, but there's no telling whose attention we caught with my light show.

I approach Caelynn slowly, heart in my throat but stomach twisting in anger.

She groans and stirs. She looks up at me through stringy blond hair all over her blood-streaked face. Her eyes are dark, eyelashes fluttering. Her energy is nearly gone entirely. Her face pale as death.

"You are going to get us both killed," I say through gritted teeth.

"Rev," she says, her voice gravelly, and she winces in pain. "I'm sorry."

But I don't dare ask her for what. I'm mad at her as tears well in my eyes. So angry for all the pain she's put me through, including this moment. Watching her die in front of me would be the greatest torture of my life.

"Don't you even trust me to be able to take care of myself? You once told me you believed in me." My head falls back, looking up to the hazy sky. "But then," I say slower, passion gone. Anger gone. Now, there is only pain. "I suppose that was a lie too."

I let that sink in for one beat before I look her in the eye. Her mouth is wide open, eyebrows scrunched. Recognition flickers in her eyes.

Will she die if I leave her now? She might. And maybe that would be a good thing. Maybe her death would free me. Maybe it's better for her too. She can live in these lands as a true wraith instead of only a pretend phantom.

"You are determined to save me, but at what point are you going to realize that I don't need it? I don't need you."

She sucks in a breath, tears filling her eyes.

Her eyes grow wide, and she squirms. I know her well enough to know this expression is not from pain.

She's scared.

Then, I feel it, the power looming over me. The air trembles around us, the light suddenly sucked from the sky.

I freeze, unable to move.

"No," Caelynn whispers, and it's her voice that breaks me from my panic-induced freeze. Slowly, I turn to face our new enemy.

It's a wraith, almost indistinguishable from the one who befriended Caelynn, except this one's smoke is lighter, a grey more than black, and there is a white light in his chest.

When he speaks, the ground rumbles beneath him. My knees nearly buckle with the weight of his words.

"Hello, little brother."

# 45
## CAELYNN

Suddenly, I am a child again. Back in the Luminescent Court palace, trapped by the High Heir, Reahgan. He holds me down with a powerful white light, and it burns every inch of my skin.

I can't move.

I can't speak.

I can't breathe.

My body is on fire with the pain of my injuries and the panic, the need to get away from him.

*Reahgan.*

*No,* I think. *No, no, no, no, no.*

I beat him. I killed him.

And he... became a wraith.

How had I not even considered that as a possibility? It makes so much sense. I always knew he was evil. He belongs here.

And so do I.

Rev is frozen before the wraith claiming to be his brother.

Coldness spreads over my body.

"You've gotten yourself into quite the predicament, brother," the smoke creature says. There is nothing distinguishable about this dark creature before us. Nothing that would pinpoint him as the late Luminescent Court heir. But I can feel it. His power, his essence.

It's him. Can Rev feel the same? And... what does that mean for him?

"Don't worry. I'll solve it all for you." His gaze shifts past Rev and onto me. "By killing *her* right here and now."

Reahgan's wraith form dissolves and rushes past Rev and straight to me. Panic swallows me whole, and my vision flickers in and out. I scramble back, but I don't have near enough control to fight him.

Reahgan in wraith form is my worst nightmare—because it's not a bad person I'm fighting. I'm not afraid of him.

I'm afraid of me.

The blackened, scarred soul in front of me is my worst moment come to life. It's the decision that both saved and ruined me.

And it's going to kill me. It's going to strangle the breath from my lungs and what little hope I held for my soul.

I'm going to die right here. Because I'm not going to stop him.

A shadow flies between us, blocking the acidic smoke that was Reahgan's attack. I cower before the magical battle swirling before me. Like storm clouds colliding in a raging war, they twist and twirl and rip at each other, crackling like thunder, but I cannot tell where one ends and the other begins.

My vision is spotted with black, and my teeth chatter. I can't feel much of anything. I can't see the fight happening over my head any longer. All I can hear is the pulse of my own heart slowing.

Then, I can feel him. A hand presses to my stomach, warm at first—then hot. Searing pain explodes over my body.

# 46
## REV

I stand there, slack-jawed as two wraiths fight like a damn hurricane over Caelynn.

What. The. Hell.

I clamber over to Caelynn's side, and my stomach sinks as I look into her unfocused eyes. She doesn't even see him. Her gaze is pinned to the two wraiths. One claiming to be her friend. One claiming to be my brother.

The shadows cast over her face makes her look like a wraith too, the haunted distant expression. Hopelessness. Fear. Pain.

Black blood bubbles from the wound in her side, caking into the dirt beneath her. It's all over her hands and even on her face. Shit, whatever is happening with her body, it's not good. And that's beside the wraiths battling over her life just feet away. Or the wall of wraiths less than a mile off, now stirring from their quiet slumber.

If I don't do something, Caelynn will die. Here. In minutes.

My stomach twists.

I don't know what to feel about her or the wraith's clashing just feet away. If that being really is my brother, maybe he deserves his vengeance. But... *it's Caelynn*. And bad or not—she's mine.

So, I allow instinct to take over. Even if it's only the magic pushing me, even if what I feel for her isn't real, I won't let this be how it ends.

I thrust my magic deep into her body, caressing every ounce of her essence. I close my eyes at how good it feels, the light that pulls at me, that fills my soul, sating the hunger deep within. The aching, the longing I've been ignoring since the day she walked into the Flicker Court before the trials. Since she walked into my life.

I throw my head back with the pleasure and warmth that fills me at this intimacy.

A familiar voice--even after all this time—breaks me from my ecstasy with a scream. "I will kill you."

The darker wraith leaps at me, his stinging power knocks me away from Caelynn.

I brace my short fall with my elbows, and I look up to see skeleton birds circling below the dark brown clouds swirling over us. And not far off, that wall of wafting wraiths is watching eagerly, drawing closer inch by inch.

"Reahgan," I say sharply. I can't wrap my mind around anything at the moment.

Could my brother possibly be a wraith? Only evil souls become wraiths in death, and my brother was not—

I shake my head, so confused, but I don't have time to think it through. I have to make a decision now. "Reahgan," I say again. "We have to go." I point to the army of shifting wraiths pressing toward us, picking up speed.

If he's my brother, in any way, I need us both to get out of here. And continuing to fight over Caelynn here in the middle of an open wraith field, is going to get us both killed—fast.

The being of light grey billowing smoke turns to the army of evil spirits, and he pauses. For a very long moment, he watches. They're rumbling toward us now. Soon, they'll be a stampede of angry souls seeking to devour us. There will be no hope of escape if we wait any longer.

His chin dips in what I assume is a nod. "Let's go," he tells me and sweeps toward the mountains away from Caelynn and her wraith.

I follow.

# 47
## CAELYNN

*oly crap.*

Wraith Reahgan and my random wraith friend just battle-royaled. Rev healed me, sending shock waves of pleasure through my whole body. Then, he left.

Or did I hallucinate all of that? That actually seems way more likely.

"Run," the gruff voice of my wraith says. "Go back to the Forest of Desires." He faces the army of wraiths roaring at us like a tsunami. "Blindfold yourself if you must, but wait there until I find you."

I suck in a breath but then scramble to my feet and follow his instruction.

Rev is gone. He ran off with Reahgan. And he wants his vengeance.

I suppose I can't blame him for that. Even if he did deserve the end he got.

The swell of wraiths rushes after me, and I sprint over the rocky plain back the way I came. They shift their trajectory away from Rev and toward me. The buzz of their eager groans grows behind me. The ground trembles beneath me, and I pick up speed, panic still thumping through my veins.

I leap into shadows, jumping ahead two dozen feet. Then, again. And again. My back still roars in pain, my limbs heavy with exhaustion, but I have enough energy for a few leaps to get ahead.

The wave of wraiths call after me. They call me by name.

*Our master wants to see you*, they say.

*Our master has a plan for you.*

*You cannot hide. You will never hide from them.*

Their words fuel me to flee even faster. Because I know who they speak of, and it's not Reahgan. It's the Night Bringer.

# 48
## REV

I sit on a dusty bed, looking around at the strange cottage smack in the middle of the Schorchedlands.

"What is this place?" I ask. I followed the wraith who claims to be my long-dead brother for a few miles over the plains and into a mountain pass. He led me down a winding path between a set of smaller mountains and straight to a very normal-looking log cottage. He had me enter and then prompted me to invite him in.

The army of wraiths kept their focus on Caelynn, which made our way fairly uneventful. But that only makes me feel guiltier. Is she okay?

Of course, she is. She's freaking Caelynn. She's amazing. She's undefeatable.

I blink as the image of her fallen body flashes before me, causing a wave of pain to rush through me.

*I healed her*, I tell myself. Not completely but enough. She'll be okay.

I take in a long breath. "Where are we?"

There is only one small room with a fireplace, rusted

pot hanging off kilter beside it. There's a small table, one window, and a bed made of straw.

Grey smoke billows from the wraith, his face unreadable. Unrecognizable. I still can't bring myself to call him by my brother's name.

"Apparently some sorcerer lived here for a few years."

I nod absently. Gavril, I remember from one of my books. "He was studying wraiths."

"He was a fool. Though, I suppose it's in your best interest. You are safe here, for now. Those wards stop spirits from entering without being invited. Making it a fairly safe abode."

I examine the glowing symbols lining the door and window of the cottage.

"Even when invited, it's rather—uncomfortable." His smoke shudders, as if illustrating that he's not feeling at his best inside these walls.

"Thanks," I say, rubbing my hands together awkwardly.

I have so many questions. Too many. My mind won't stop on just one, I'm overwhelmed.

"So..." I begin but trail off.

The wraith chuckles. "So, brother. You've taken up with my murderer, have you?"

I blink. Oh, we're going there, are we?

"Not that I blame you. She's quite attractive. I'd have bedded her myself if given the chance. I simply would have killed her *after*."

My stomach sinks, the breath leaves my lungs. *No. No, this is not my brother.*

I close my eyes but can't get the image from the Orb of

Terrors out of my head. Reahgan holding Caelynn down with his magic and touching her...

"How do I even know you're my brother?" I spit.

He chuckles. "Sorry, brother. I forget you were always the honorable one. The bleeding heart, making friends with those of low birth and even the servants." His smoky shoulders rise in a shrug.

"You weren't like this," I whisper. "You were..."

"Good?"

I nod.

"Perhaps. For a time. But it's much easier to become a wraith than you'd think. If you continue focusing all your energy on your hatred for my murderer, you'll find yourself joining me here in your afterlife. If you had died in the trials like he wanted, you and I would have been reunited several weeks sooner."

"I don't know if I believe you."

He sighs, smoky arms flailing around as he spins. Reahgan always was the dramatic one. "Well, let me put it this way: would another wraith put himself at risk to save you? I protected you against Father while I lived and against my own kind here, now. They'll be hunting you, even now."

"Then, why didn't they follow us?"

"Because she is more important. You are a secondary mission." He floats around the room like he can't manage to sit still. "Their master has other plans for the shadow bitch. They are ordered to capture her and take her straight to the devil."

"The Night Bringer?"

"Ha! The Night Bringer is not in this cursed place. He

couldn't leave if he ever entered. That's the problem, you see." He shakes his head. "No, the Night Bringer was your devil. The Night Terror is ours."

I sit up straighter.

"One monster of ancient renown is inside the Schorchedlands. The other outside. And they will do anything to be together again."

I blink and shake my head. There's another one. I recall the voice that attempted to lure me inside the caves during the trials. How Caelynn pulled me back. That's my only experience with the beings in question. But I don't need to know more than that hypnosis, the cascade of dark power that held me captive for those few moments—and the look of fear in her eyes. Caelynn, my powerful and brave and bold shadow fae, is petrified of him.

And now, I learn there are two.

"Father must be so pleased that you made it inside these walls," Reahgan chuckles. "You're strong, brother. He wished you to be weak, but the more you proved him wrong, the angrier he became."

The wraith drifts toward the bed and settles over it as if pretending to sit like a living being. He's not alive. And yet, he's here. His soul, trapped in this place.

"I'm proud of you, Rev."

I swallow. "Is it really you?" My heart aches. I want it to be him, so badly. And yet, it boggles my mind. Maybe I shouldn't wish it.

The wraith's face softens if such an expression is even possible for a creature made entirely of magic. He places a smoke hand onto my forearm. "Look inside," he says softly. "You'll see everything you need."

I turn toward his swirling body and look into the light at his chest. It's bright white, like a pure ball of luminescent energy. The light swells and then covers everything.

I am a child again, running through the iridescent forest after my older brother, Reahgan. He's so much faster. He slips through the trees and tricks me. He tosses a pile of glittering leaves over my head and laughs, running the other way.

I pull away from the wraith, blinking rapidly. My heart swells, feeling his essence.

*It is him. This is my brother.*

Bile rises in my throat.

"I was not always the best brother, Reveln. But I did love you. I still do."

I swallow and close my eyes. My brother. My idol. My hero. My role model.

Is... a wraith.

"You are not a prince, you never were. But though our fathers are different fae, we share a mother. That makes you my brother. That makes you mine. And I will always fight for what is mine."

"Mine," I whisper. But it's not Reahgan's face that drifts through my mind. I blink the image back. "Tell me everything you know, Reahgan." His name is foreign on my lips.

He wrinkles his nose like it's an inconvenience to him. "You have a destiny, but she has a bigger one." His voice is bored. This is no longer about his glory, his purpose. This is about mine and my mate's. I narrow my eyes, attempting to read his expression—though on a wraith that's rather challenging. "You can heal the land," his voice lowers.

Displeased, I guess. "She will curse it. Caelynn, and Caelynn alone, has the ability to destroy the walls that keep souls bound to this place." His voice rises. He enjoys this part. He watches my expression in return, eyes lighting as a flicker of pain passes through me.

He enjoys my pain.

I believe him when he says he loves me. That he'll fight for me. But he desires power for himself. No one else. Especially his little brother.

"It wasn't revenge that drove me to kill her in the valley, Reveln. It was this. She must die, or else those monsters will use her to escape this place. And if the Night Terror and the Night Bringer are reunited, no one can stand against them."

# 49
## CAELYNN

The wraiths halt right at the edge of the Forest of Desires. At least my wraith friend was right about this place—it's safe from my most pressing threat, the wraiths.

Too bad it's creepy. As. Hell.

Music plays from within the treeline, soft and melodic. It's the song Rev and I danced to the first time we met. Before either of us knew who the other was.

So, even though I refuse to look through the trees to see young Rev watching me with those big silver eyes, or offering me a glass of bubbling red wine, or kissing me beneath the soft luminescent light of the ballroom, I still picture all of it in my mind.

Part of me wants to give in and fantasize about one of my only good memories. The other is terrified I'll lose myself to the hypnosis of this place.

I've seen enough to know that I definitely do not want to die here. I do not want to be eaten alive by evil trees or join the thousands of souls within their trunks and limbs —no matter how lovely the images they show me are.

So, I light a fire, and I stare into the flames, remembering who I am. What I am. And what I'm here for. I don't know where Rev is or how to get to him now, I don't know if he's in trouble or if I can save him, but I'm sure as hell going to try. And those evil spirits in this forest will not stop me.

It's almost sundown when my wraith finally shows back up. He pushes through some barriers I hadn't seen before.

I leap to my feet as he reaches me. "Where the hell have you been?" I shout rudely.

"Shhhh," he purrs. "You'll wake the dead, honey."

I roll my eyes. "The dead are very much awake."

He smiles.

"You have some explaining to do," I say, sitting back down next to my fire. I cross my arms dramatically. But I do still have a lot of questions. I start with the simplest first. "How can you enter this forest but the others can't?"

"Oh, they can but they choose not to. Wraiths are not admirers of this place. And those spirits do not have sufficient motivation to find you. Otherwise, they'd be here. By morning, they'll forget you were ever here, to begin with."

I shake my head. Those are the mindless wraiths he'd mentioned. The ones with no hope left, that don't remember who they are or have any desires of their own anymore. They wander aimlessly.

They only attacked me because we brought attention to ourselves, and they desire to kill any living being in their lands. Except...

"They said things to me. Called to me by name..."

The wraith stills but doesn't speak. I absently pick at the pebbles on the ground beside the fire.

"There has been a message floating through the Schorchedlands for weeks now. Every wraith knows to look for you. That is why they followed you and not your lover. You are the priority."

I swallow.

"Then, wouldn't they come after me, even if it were uncomfortable? If there's a bounty on my head..."

"Not these wraiths. But others, yes. And it isn't on your head. No, the Night Terror made it very clear that she wants you alive. You alive and Rev dead."

I cover my mouth with my hand. "The Night Bringer still wants him dead."

"Yes," the wraith whispers. "He's always wanted him dead. But you are more important, and Rev is your weakness. He kept him alive, often against his pet, the Luminescent Court King's desires, so that he'd be able to use him against you."

I nod. Not even caring that it's been working. All of it. He plopped it in my mind that Rev was in trouble, and I immediately came running, exactly where he wanted me.

"Why does he want me here?"

The wraith wafts for a moment, his bottom half swaying in the wind, then he spins and sits beside me. "Let me tell you a story," he says, then he points into the woods over my shoulder. "The forest shows me what I desire too. A few of our desires are the same. A powerful Shadow Court stronghold. A strong queen able to build it back up into a mighty force. Those are things I could still see come to fruition. Things I could still make happen, through you."

I bite my lip. I do want those things too, but they are so far away now. How I could even think to hope for it?

"But the forest usually shows me darker desires. The ones I've lost forever. It shows me what will never be."

I look into the woods and ignore the lovely young couple dancing fluidly and find a rocking chair. A lovely young female rocks a baby in her arms.

"That is my son," the wraith says. "History will tell you that he did not live past his sixth birthday."

I swallow. "I'm sorry."

"But that is a lie. You see, I was forced to give him up."

I suck in a breath as the image changes, the boy grows into a child running through the Whisperwood. "Why?"

"I was the king of the Shadow Court, and my child was too strong."

My mouth falls open.

"If I hadn't sent him away to live as my cousin's son, he would have been taken from me. My own father would have killed him, if given the chance."

I shake my head, not understanding.

"My father had been High King, the last Shadow Court High Ruler. And during his time, there was a war. Again, history will lie to you and tell you that the High King tried to use his powerful court to keep power longer than his one hundred years. They'd tell you it was a civil war, court against court. But that is a falsehood. Our opponent was a pair of ancient beings. These beings are old and powerful, nearly unbeatable. They have their own stories and histories that go back millennia. We can't even pretend to know enough about them to understand who they are or where they come from, or even what they want. But I know them to be two of the most evil creatures ever to walk our realm."

"The Night Bringer?" I ask in a whisper.

"Yes. The Night Bringer was one."

"But there's another."

The wraith nods slowly. He sniffs, watching the forest and the child running away from him.

"The only way we could win the battle was to trick the beings. We had one secret weapon: another being like them. She was powerful enough to cast a spell, binding them to one area forever."

My eyebrows pull down.

"We succeeded in trapping one of the two beings. If I had been able to get them both—if the Night Bringer hadn't figured it out just in time—we wouldn't have had to dismantle my court. I wouldn't have had to give away my own child, hide him away."

"What does your son have to do with it?"

"Well, the spell that bound the Night Terror to the Schorchedlands was cast by two beings. One was that ancient ally I mentioned, and the other—me. It cannot be reversed without one of the two of us. The guardian will not bend and so the Night Terror cannot leave these cursed lands unless someone of my own blood with a very large amount of shadow power casts the reversal spell."

"So your son..."

He nods. "My son had the ability to reverse the spell, and I knew the Night Bringer would come for him. So, I hid him away. No one knew where he went. The few I confided in, I told that I'd sent him to another court—he was young enough that he would adapt to the new element he was placed into. He'd no longer be a shadow fae and would no longer be able to pass down the power needed to reverse the curse. The next several High Kings called us weak and began the political war that would eventually bring our incredible court to its knees. And my father let them because he didn't trust me. He helped them by selling off children to other courts, weakening us. He must have known I'd kept my heir somewhere in the shadow lands because he pushed all of the most powerful children away."

I suck in a breath. I knew females in my court had been forced into marriage in other courts. I knew this was to keep us weak. But I'd always thought it was because the other courts feared us and our power.

He's telling me—it was for the good of the world.

"My father and the High Counsel knew the weaker we were, the less likely there would ever rise a child able to break the curse. Those are deeds I was never able to forgive. Deeds that drove me mad in my living years."

"He was trying to save the world... by dismantling his own kingdom." My heart aches at this story. What would I have done, in this situation? I try putting myself in his place. And I... don't think I could have done it. It's like breaking your own child's leg because being able-bodied would put them at risk. It's still not right. It's cruel and unfair.

"And, perhaps, he was right. Because it almost worked." He nods again to the forest. Where the image of his son as a boy shifts into an adult with a child of his own.

And that child grows, to have her own. And that child grows to have his own.

"The Shadow Court passed to a new ruling family, another cousin chosen by my father, and my line was lost to all but me. I watched them from afar. Each child of my line I knew was at risk, but they grew weaker and weaker thanks to my father's work."

I narrow my eyes as one of the boys grows into a shadow fae I recognize.

"Until the Night Bringer got his hands on one of my children's children's children, and he died in the process of casting the spell. He wasn't strong enough. Hundreds of years passed, and I'd thought it was over. There would never again exist a shadow fae with both the power and blood needed."

A baby appears in the familiar fae's arms. She gets bigger, her hair grows long and blond. Her eyes are big and golden, lovely but not very bright.

The blond shadow fae grows until she's like looking in a mirror.

"Until me."

# 50
## REV

I lean over, hands a tight fist in my hair.

"But what about the spellbook?" I ask my brother in wraith form.

I continue to struggle between loving the soul of my lost brother and the realization that he's not who I thought he was. He never was.

It means what I saw in the Orb of Terrors of what he did to Caelynn was likely true. And it means when she said he deserved to die...

I shake my head from those thoughts. I'd prayed—begged—so many times for a chance to talk to my brother again. One more time.

Now, I'm getting that chance to do it. It's just... not at all what I was hoping for.

"What about it?" Reahgan asks, exasperated. He always did get annoyed with me so quickly.

"The High Queen sent me here to get the spellbook because it has the cure to the scourge inside it."

Reahgan begins a hysterical laugh. "So, the queen is in

on this too. My! How elaborate this plan was. The Night Bringer has certainly been working overtime.”

“The queen… in on it?” I mumble.

“Oh, my sweet, naive little brother.” He’s pleased he knows more than I do. “The only thing in that spellbook is the means to unbind the Night Terror from her cell inside these cursed walls.”

“What?”

“Would you come up with something more intelligent to say than *what*?”

I groan.

“The point of all of this, Rev, is that your damaged lover cannot get her hands on that book. We cannot allow it to happen.”

“I can’t let you kill Caelynn,” I say with more force than I’d yet had toward my brother. The words surprise even me.

He grows still. “Excuse me?”

“I don’t know as much as you do about the scourge and this Night Terror, but I’m not going to let you hurt her.”

Reahgan chuckles. It’s softer than before, but if there is one thing I know about my brother—when he gets quiet, he’s angry. “She sure has got her claws in you deep.”

“That’s not true. I hate her. But I still…”

“You hate her,” he repeats, dumbfounded. “You hate her, but you will betray your own brother to save her life?”

“Stop,” I say, pressing my fists to my eyes.

Reahgan circles me, examining me like a wild animal caught in a trap. “It’s the magic of the mating bond,” he says definitively. “Yes. If you mean it, that you hate her, yet you’d say those things…”

He presses his face close to mine, and I squirm back, avoiding looking right into the black void where his eyes should be.

"Then, you are simply being manipulated by the magic of the bond. Your feelings for her are not real, little brother. It will convince you to protect her at all costs, even when it makes no sense."

"No," I say, even though I've had those same thoughts. Where does the mating bond begin and I end? What's real, and what's the magic? That, I don't know.

Reahgan drifts to the floor beside me, hands on my knee and face inches from mine. The smell of burnt flesh fills my nose. "I can cure you," he whispers seriously. "I can break the bond."

My eyes fly open. "What?"

"The bond is simply a spell. And it can be broken." He rushes over the words like he's just figuring this all out along with me. "You can be free of this spell she has on you. You'd be able to see so clearly then!"

My stomach sinks. I don't want that—do I? My feelings for Caelynn are so complicated it would be nice to be able to sift through them easier. But *breaking* the bond?

"You are so easy to manipulate, and she's doing it to you now. I won't let them win this game just because of your sappy feelings that aren't even authentic."

"This isn't a game, Reahgan."

"To them it is! They want to destroy us all. And they're moving naïve and ignorant living fae—like you—around like fucking chess pieces. It's masterful, really."

I don't know what to believe. His story fits.

But he wants to kill Caelynn because he thinks she's going to help the Night Bringer destroy the world.

"Even if all of this is true, Caelynn would need to cast the spell. She won't do it."

"That's what you're putting your bets on, Rev? That your sweet fated mate will refuse to do their bidding? How do you think I died, Rev? She killed me to complete a bargain she made with them!"

"What did you do to her?" I say as those images play through my head again. Caelynn held down by my brother's power. Nausea rolls through me.

While he was alive, I'd always hero-worshiped my brother. So much I hadn't seen the cruelty in his eyes.

But I see it now.

"Before Caelynn killed you. What did you do to her?"

"Ha!" he spits. "I did nothing to her."

"I saw you." I stand. "You held her down."

"She was an assassin! A spy sent to kill my little brother. What did you expect me to do? Pour her tea? No, I was going to do whatever was required to get answers from her."

"You enjoyed it." It feels right, this realization. He'd always liked causing others pain. He reveled in it. The way he picked on me wasn't just a big brother teasing his sibling. He loved it. He liked seeing my tears. My pain.

"I didn't do anything. The bitch broke free of my holding before I had the chance."

I shoot a blast of white-hot power straight into the wraith's chest, and he crashes through the far wall, wood splintering. Anger fills me, and I charge my brother.

# 51
## CAELYNN

Soft moans--a mixture of pleasure and pain—drift through the dark trees. The sun has set entirely now, leaving the space between the white tree trunks pitch black. I couldn't see their haunting images even if I allowed myself to look.

But now, the voices are louder.

It seems the forest has shifted its strategy with less to show and more to tell.

*Caelynn*, a myriad of voices whisper. So many of them, calling to me. *Lead us, Caelynn. Be our queen. Give us our power back.*

I swallow. *Not real.*

"That's why the Night Bringer gave me his power," I say, running my new truths through my mind. "It wasn't some benevolent act for a fae doing his bidding." I take in a huge breath and hold it. This... this story is too much. It twists all the things I thought I knew into something entirely different.

"It all served a purpose," my wraith agrees.

I let out my breath slowly. "If all of this is true..."

"You are the one they've been waiting for. They need you to free them."

I shake my head. Yes, sure that's true, but there's more. Maybe in the grand scheme of things, it shouldn't matter. Maybe the evil plot to destroy the world is more important, but my mind is caught on two important facts.

"It means I'm your great, great, great, great... granddaughter."

The wraith grows still. "Yes," he whispers.

"It means... it means I have royal blood."

"Yes."

I blink slowly. The Night Bringer once told me that if I did as he told me, I'd become Queen of the Shadow Court. All I needed was his power and the freedom to choose my own court. Those two things he would give me, and even without any more involvement, the Queen of the Whisperwood would name me her heir. The Shadow Court needs a strong ruler. And I would be the only one in the entire kingdom with the power to fuel it all.

So, the possibility of being the Queen of the Shadow Court is not new. It was never really a possibility because I was banished quickly after I earned my magic. But the thought, the vague hope, was always there. Since I was an adolescent.

But this... this is something different. This is destiny. This is a life that was taken from me.

I should have been a princess.

That throne isn't just a vague possibility out of coincidence and convenience. It's rightfully *mine*.

I shake my head as all the things I learned swirl

through my mind. Wraiths are not traditionally very trust-worthy allies—unless you've bound them to a bargain, which I haven't. So, all of this could be bull shit. It could be more manipulation. God knows I've had my fair share of that.

But the forest's images do not lie. So, I can trust that, somehow, I am part of his desires. And it's very clear to me that this means a lot to him. This wraith feels strongly about this story. About me.

So, maybe it's only partially true. But I don't really care.

I take in a long breath, accepting everything he's said as truth. "I'm going to kill him."

"Yes! Now, you understand!" The wraith floats in the air, his bottom half swishing eagerly. "Rev must die so that you can live to restore the Shadow—"

"No," I say. "I will kill the Night Terror. I will kill the Night Bringer's mate so he knows what it feels like."

He stops, eyeing me carefully.

"Rev will live," I tell him. "He will be the hero the realm needs. And he'll go on to be High King."

"But... then you will still be imprisoned here. Forever. And our court will fall. You are the last heir. The last one. Do you understand what that means?"

"It means we're no worse off than before. No one knew I existed. " I shrug.

His mouth falls open. "I thought you loved our court. I thought you'd fight for it, choose it, above all else."

I nod slowly. "I'd choose it above all else. Except him."

If I'd known all of this before... before the trials, before my time with him in the Crumbling Court, before crushing his heart to help—maybe I'd have chosen differently.

No, I cannot kill him because my own choices backed me into a corner. I am not that selfish.

I turn and face the fire, flickering gently in the darkness. My wraith—my ancestor—doesn't make a sound, and I don't turn to face him. I'd leave now if I didn't know it was certain death to cross the plains at night. I must wait for the morning.

So, I wait, contemplating my entire life with this new information. Did my father know? That would make a lot of sense actually. And my Gran too.

It's why they wanted to send me away. It's why they thought my disobedience put me in danger. It's why they feared me after I'd killed Reahgan. It's why they pushed to have me banished. Because I had this dark power now that was dangerous to the whole realm.

Eventually, I slip into a fitful sleep, and when I wake ready to set off over the now vacant wraith plains to find Rev, my wraith is gone. Maybe he left the moment I chose Rev over his vendetta. I don't care. My mind is made up.

I choose Rev.

I will always choose him.

———

The plains are as empty and open as they were yesterday morning. Though, of course, I know better. An army of wraiths waits in the shadows for any hint of Rev or me.

I suppose it should be a relief to know they don't want me dead. They just want to capture and take me to the Night Terror. Except, I'd take death over torture any day.

*Death would be a mercy*. That's what my magic whispered in my ear those days I was bound by a bargain to the Night Bringer.

I cover myself in shadow. It would be preferable for me to save my magic for more important things than staying hidden, but after yesterday, I know this is a worthy use of my magic. It doesn't take much anyway. I'll just keep my shadow leaping to a minimum.

I take off at a full sprint across the plains. I find the massive footprints of the zombie bear and the dirt scorched from Rev's magic, but the bear's lifeless carcass is nowhere to be found. I keep running. After a few miles and no surprising mishaps, I reach the looming shadow of the mountain pass. I don't know where Reahgan took Rev, but I know where Rev will be heading eventually—through this mountain pass and deeper into the Schorchedlands.

I slow to walk when the ground beneath me shifts from ashy dirt to uneven rubble and stone. When light from the hazy sky is completely blocked from view by the massive mountains.

There are a few leafless trees here but no water sources. I'm already running low on water, but now isn't the time to worry about that. I have to find Rev first. Figure out how to not die of thirst second—or at least somewhere on my to-do list.

I continue walking slowly, shadows still covering me, but a soft glow appears between two smaller mountains.

The glow recedes like nothing had been out of place at all.

On a whim, I follow the pathway toward the light. It's winding, passing through a few small nooks between a set of mountains, and uphill. Finally, I turn a corner and suck in a breath at a tiny cottage smack in the middle of a red-tinted valley.

A fucking cottage in the middle of the Schorchedlands.

Now, even if this has nothing to do with Rev—I've got to find out what the hell is up with this place.

# 52
## REV

Reahgan's smoky form rises from the blackened dirt outside the cottage, shattered glass, and splintered wood scattered at his feet.

"You see! You can't think straight about her!" His booming voice rumbles the ground beneath me as I walk around to face him. "You'd attack me, your own brother, over the whore who killed me?"

My chest heaves. Around a hundred feet behind Reahgan is a swamp of bubbling black fluid. What lies inside the blackened water? More bones eager to devour me or something else? Something worse.

"I can free you of that burden," he purrs as his body again floats to the air.

My chest heaves. "I don't want to harm you," I say, ignoring his comment.

"No? You just blasted me through the stupid cottage in rage. Defending the honor of your whore of a mate."

"Stop!" I yell. "Stop calling her that."

Reahgan laughs again, and the rocky terrain around us

rumbles. "You are farther under her spell than I thought. A sick puppy in love with the shadow bitch!"

Reahgan laughs maniacally as I charge him, fists swinging. I fly straight through his body and skid to a stop on the other side.

"You cannot harm me with your fists, brother," he shouts, sick amusement in his voice. "And if you use your magic, you'll draw the wraiths to you"

"Ahhh, look—the wraiths are already on their way." Smoke like acid stings in my ear as he dissolves around me.

Behind Reahgan, a shadow soars straight at me. So fast, so close. I wince, but instead of me, it slams right into my brother. The collision sizzles like water on coals.

The shadow shifts into a blond fae with her hand around Reahgan's throat, black flames licking over her skin. She slams him against the wall of the cottage.

Reahgan groans quietly, his smoke flickering.

"Don't you dare touch him," Caelynn spits.

"He attacked me," Reahgan says with a weak voice.

"The wards," I say. Caelynn partially turns toward me. I don't dare question how she found us here. That's the least of my concerns right now. "The house has wards to keep the wraiths away, and it hurts him."

Caelynn presses his harder against the door. "Good to know."

Reahgan lets out a withering cry, but it morphs into a laugh. With a crash like a bull, I'm thrust onto the ground. "Kill!" a voice hisses at me. A new wraith, charcoal grey, wiggles over me, eager to have claimed a prize.

Caelynn drops my brother and turns to face our new

threat. She throws her black flame at the wraith over me, but he's quickly replaced by two more.

Three wraiths have approached from the mountainside, eager to spill my blood. Reahgan was right—my magic did draw them.

*Master has called.*

*She's waiting for you.*

"Get inside the house!" I call to her. I throw up a wall of white light between us and the wooden door. We both sprint toward the safety of the warded cottage.

I slam the door shut behind us and press my weight against it. My chest heaves up and down as I press my back against the very small barrier between us.

The attack began as only three wraiths, but how many more will be after us? I picture the army from the plains and shudder. Even with ward magic, I can't imagine this cottage could withstand such an attack.

I've never heard of wraiths hunting someone the way they're apparently hunting us. It's part of the "plot" Caelynn uncovered, but even so it seems... odd.

The mountains rumble around us.

Hysterical laughter fills the house, and the overcast face of a wraith appears in the shattered window.

"Would you look at who decided to show up," Reahgan purrs. "Now, it's my turn to save my ungrateful brother and the world all in one violent murder."

My brother chuckles, and Caelynn shudders beside me.

"Reahgan, stop this." I have a lot of conflicting feelings about Caelynn, but I do not want her dead. I haven't for months now. She's already doomed herself, sacrificed herself, in a misguided attempt to save me. She doesn't need to die too.

"Why would my death save him?" Caelynn asks suddenly through heavy breaths.

Reahgan's body simmers into a liquid form as he seeps through the small window and his body reforms besides the rusty pans.

"Ah, I see now." Reahgan tilts his head curiously as he flutters toward us casually. "I'd thought us two eternal enemies, fated to always battle, but we've found something in common."

I purse my lips. What—

"Our love for Reveln," Reahgan says.

It's hard for me to imagine a wraith loving anything at all, but this is my brother. The tattered remains of my brother's soul.

"So, let me explain, my dear, and perhaps we can come to an arrangement."

"Stop this, Reahgan." Chills cascade down my spine. I don't like this conversation at all. "I don't care what plot you've uncovered; unnecessary death is never okay."

"Oh! But it is necessary. And I think your lover will agree."

"How does my death save him?" Caelynn says firmly through gritted teeth.

I turn my gaze to hers, pleading. She can't possibly be considering... "Caelynn, he's manipulating you."

But her stare doesn't leave my brother's. Outside the walls of this little cottage, the eager moans of wraiths fill the valley. I swallow.

"The Night Terror needs you," Reahgan says in a

pleased, singsong tone. This is a game to him. He's enjoying it. "He requires you alive and Rev dead. If you were to die, all hopes of his plan are lost. Rev will be of no consequence to him any longer."

My gaze darts between them—Caelynn is considering his words carefully, still fully ignoring me. Reahgan wafts gently, almost dancing beneath the short ceiling of the wooden building.

"He'll still kill him for spite."

"True, but the Night Terror is trapped inside the deepest parts of the Schorchedlands. She has sent messages to all the corners of this place, so all the spirits know you. They know that you are the key to their freedom. They won't live again, but they can be free within the living world. All they need is you captured and my brother dead. If I were to succeed in my mission to kill you before that happens, I could feasibly get Reveln out before the Night Terror reaches him. And there will be no reason for them to continue the hunt."

"No!" I yell. Are they both this insane? Don't they understand how hard I worked to get here? Between the trials and the months I spent desperate to figure out how to get through the Wicked Gates... they think I'd throw it all away because a few wraiths are after me? Or even because there is an ancient being who wants me dead? "I am not leaving without the cure!"

"There is no cure, you fool!" Reahgan yells. "It's all a farce. You can leave here and save the world by using that magical healing power of yours."

"He's right," Caelynn whispers.

"What?" What the hell does she know that I don't?

"I mean I don't know about your healing powers but... there are apparently other ways to cure the scourge." She bites her lip. "The spellbook—they need it and me—to break the binding on the Night Terror and set her free. That was always the plan. That was the reason for the trials, for all of it. They used us."

"No," I say again.

"Enough useless talk," Reahgan says as he leaps straight at the incredibly beautiful blond fae beside me. Panic rushes through my body as Reahgan's clawed hand forces its way through Caelynn's chest, just below her sternum, and she cries out in agony.

The pain must be immense, but she doesn't try to stop him even as bright red blood splatters against the walls.

"NO!" I scream again.

I blast my blinding light at my wraith brother. With trembling fingers, Caelynn thrusts open the door and sprints into the valley where three wraiths are waiting for us.

"She is going to die, brother."

My breath comes out shaky.

"Let me break the mating bond first. Then, you won't feel the pain of it."

I shake my head. I will feel the pain of it no matter how I lose her.

I only wish I knew how to tell what's magic and what's real.

# 53
## CAELYNN

Tears sting my eyes as I run headfirst into three startled wraiths. They call me by name. *Caelynn. The Night Bringer's pet. Come with us. Become one of us.*

Oh, I intend to.

Because Reahgan was right. Entirely right. My death will ensure Rev's survival.

Victory and defeat in the same moment. That right there is the story of my life.

The Night Bringer and his apparent lover will be foiled. She'll be trapped inside these cursed walls forever. And it will ensure the falling of the Shadow Court.

If I die... it's all over. The good and the bad.

I'm trapped here anyway. There's no escape for me from this place, so why not begin my life as a wraith earlier than planned?

I run past the wraiths, straight to the edge of the bubbling pit of muck. Then, I face them. They won't kill me, that's the problem. I need to die for this to work. Or I'll risk the Night Bringer winning this game of will and wit. I will not let him win.

I will not let him, or his comrade, get his claws into me again. With my last breath, I will fight him. Literally. I'll give my last breath to ensure their loss.

"Reahgan!" I call out. The other wraiths come floating up slowly, calling to me. Saying my name over and over and over again. "I'll make a bargain with you, Reahgan."

# 54
## REV

Reahgan chuckles lightly. "It sounds as if your lover is prepared to die."

He turns from me and soars out the jagged glass that had been a window. I rush out the door, but the three other wraiths are surrounding Caelynn. They have her pinned between them and the black swamp.

They call to her. *Come with us. Come.*

"No," she tells them. "I have other plans."

In her eyes is a resolve like I've never seen. What the hell is she doing?

"Get back inside the house, Rev," she yells. "It's the only safe place."

"What's your bargain, dear?" Reaghan asks.

"Get them away from me, and we'll discuss."

My brother's wraith twists in delight, a sick dance of smoking limbs.

"Get the male," Reahgan demands of the wayward wraiths. Their eyes are unfocused. "I'll get the girl. We've come to an... understanding."

The slack-jawed wraiths pause as if considering, but finally, one prowls toward me, and the other two follow.

Then, with a smile that chills my spine, my brother's broken soul turns toward Caelynn.

Caelynn who isn't even holding a weapon.

I need to stop whatever is happening between them. They're both my allies, and yet, I know them working together will only result in a shattered heart on my end. I'm supposed to hate her. I'm supposed to want her dead.

Maybe it's only the mating magic talking but... I don't have time to think it all through before the wayward wraiths are on me.

The darkest of the three collides with me; his touch burns like hellfire, sending my whole body into convulsions. I scream but manage to send a jolt of magic to toss him back. He hisses in pain, but the next grasps my throat in his greedy hands. My iron knife slices through his limbs, but he's replaced by the next. One after the other. Slap, a punch, slice, all defended one after the other, but I'm not fast enough. My magic dissolves one into ash. It's easier than I expected to fell him but now their every blow comes faster and stronger, and every defensive move comes slower and weaker.

Then, it's her scream that fills my ears. *Caelynn.*

Everything in my body reacts, and it hurts so much worse than anything the wraiths could do to me. She's dying.

*Caelynn is dying.*

The wraiths attacking me seem to have the same thought, and they rush to where my brother stands over her limp body, blood pooling at his smoky legs.

*No.*

I pool my energy into one blast and let my rage be my guide as I blast it from my body like a grenade. The wraiths hiss in agony, and I sprint past them toward her.

My mate. My enemy. My heart, dark and broken. But mine all the same.

Another wave of magic knocks Reahgan from her fallen body, and I can't think anymore. I can only feel the panic coursing through my body.

*Not her. Not now. Not like this.*

Caelynn's long eyelashes flutter as I fall to my knees beside her. There is a gaping hole in her stomach oozing black. A hole my brother put there. She wheezes with every breath, her eyes staring straight up into the hazy sky.

She will never leave this place. She will never have hope or love again.

The wraiths scream, their power rumbles the ground beneath her. Her. Mine. Reahgan chuckles but stands between us. More wraiths appear over the mountainside, approaching quickly. Hunting me. Stalking her.

"You did this on purpose," I say to my fallen mate.

"Rev," she says.

She keeps doing this. She keeps making these sacrifices —for me. So long ago, she killed my brother and lost her freedom just to save me. She fought battles she shouldn't have been able to win to save my life in the trials—when I wanted nothing more than to strangle her with my bare hands. She gave up the win for me.

She gave up the chance to see her own kingdom for the first time to help me.

*I liked it,* her voice rings in my ear. I believed her. But seeing her now. The expression on her face when Reahgan first showed up. The adoration in her dying eyes as she looks at me now. I wanted an excuse to push her away because it was easier.

Easier than this hopeless desperation. Easier than letting her go, knowing she was everything I'd ever desired in a lover. Beautiful and strong and bold and brave.

But I don't believe her anymore.

I forgave her for a sin I'd thought unforgivable—until she'd used that very thing to push me away. Why did she do that if it wasn't true?

My stomach twists as my mind leaps to the wraith's riddle. *What is the quest every soul takes up when they enter the Schorchedlands?*

"Why do you keep doing this? Choose yourself, just once," I beg her as I press my hand to her stomach. The black liquid burns my skin.

"I'll always choose you." She wheezes.

My fingers flash with warmth, my magic pulsing, already stitching her together from the inside out. Her back arches, her eyes shut, and she lets out a magnificent groan. A moan that heats me from the inside. Dammit, now is not the time to think of her that way.

"You see, your magic acts without your permission," Reahgan says calmly. I pull my hand away and swallow, glancing back at the scene behind me. Apparently, those three wraiths were no match for my brother. They are all but ash scattered on the ground. But there are more lining the mountain passes, staring down at us. It's only a matter of time until they join the fray.

Reahgan always was the strongest of us all.

Except Caelynn.

Caelynn was always stronger.

I look down at her, checking her health. Red blood still pours from her open wound, the pain still sketched across her face. But she'll live, at least for a little while longer. I have time to figure this out first.

"Let's finish what we agreed to in the cottage," he says, approaching slowly like I'm a wild animal he's afraid to spook. He stands over us both.

Caelynn's eyes grow wide.

"Give me your hand, and I'll break the mating bond."

Caelynn gasps, and my stomach sinks.

"You'll be free of her curse, brother. You'll see clearly," Reahgan adds patiently. Always the older brother, looking to teach me something new.

I did want it…. Because I'm so confused about what is real and what is just the magic. I turn back to Caelynn, and her eyes are… indescribable. Pain like I've never seen before.

I've seen fear in her eyes before, but not like this. This time, it's pure devastation. "No," she breathes. "Please."

My breaths become labored, my heart aching. I could break the bond with her. I could clear my head, and maybe Reahgan's right—I'd see clearly then.

But then, maybe I wouldn't. Maybe I'd still love her and hate her and need her without magic telling me so.

"I've already given everything," she begs. "Please, don't take that." Her body is beaten and battered, her blood slick on my hands.

"Pathetic child," my brother complains. "Stop your whining."

My eyebrows pinch together. "The things you said to me in the shadow room at the High Court."

She winces, and her face falls more, as if resigning to her fate. Her lips press together, and a sob shudders her shoulders.

"Did you only say those things," I continue softly. I have to know. "Because you knew breaking my heart, pushing me away, was the only way to get me through the Wicked Gates?"

*Their single worst sin becomes the soul's new quest. Resolve it, and be redeemed.*

My hatred of her, my rage—that was my flaw. My weakness. My damnation. And I'd forgiven her. Is that why I couldn't enter the Schorchedlands? And is that why she said it?

"Rev," my brother says more forcefully.

Caelynn's eyes pop back open, gold flickering for only a moment. "Yes," she whispers desperately.

I nod; that truth settles easily. It all fits, all makes sense. It's so within Caelynn's character to destroy things, especially herself, to save me.

My brother, the brother I mourned for a decade, whose death I never got over, is standing by me, ready to fight with me. For me. He's ready to take my hand and help me become High King, the position stripped from him by the very female dying in my arms.

But I won't take more from her. I won't let her keep giving all of herself for me.

This time, it won't be Caelynn breaking herself for me.

This time, I'll break myself—for her.

I stand and face my brother, hands clenched into tight fists.

## 55

## CAELYNN

I can't breathe as I look up at Rev's glowing hands grip his brother's throat. Reahgan roars in rage and pain, writhing in agony.

"No," Rev says, his voice husky and determined.

My heart throbs in my chest. I squirm, but I can't move. He healed me enough that I'm not currently dying like I'd planned, but my body is still broken. Shattered.

"Please!" Reahgan begs, his expression falling into desperation as Rev's magic grows hotter, stronger. Even the wraiths on the edges of the valley have paused, watching his luminescent power light up the miles around us. Wraiths do not like the light.

"Let me kill her, and it'll be all over," Reahgan begs. "You can go home, heal the world with your father's magic, and become king."

"You and I both know it's not that simple," Rev says, pushing his brother farther back, away from me. "You don't want to kill her for *me*. None of it was ever for me. It was all for you. Everything you ever did was selfish, only to put yourself ahead."

"You're a naive fool, little brother!"

"Not anymore."

"Fine," he says through clenched teeth, between whines of pain and panting breaths. "If killing the bitch that murdered me will save the world, then you damn well better believe I'm ready and willing to tear her limb from limb."

I suck in a breath as Rev presses the iron blade to his brother's chest, right where the white light flickers inside his smoky body. He's going to kill him. Destroy his soul for good.

"How dare you?" Reahgan screams. "You would choose her over your own brother? You would choose my murderer? The fae who will destroy everything you've ever loved."

"Yes," he says, but his determination falters. "I choose her."

# 56
## REV

"I will kill you if I have to," I tell Reahgan, pressing the iron blade tighter to his soul, and I mean it. Although, I'll do everything in my power to avoid it. He is my brother, and evil or not I do love him.

"You think she is better than me? You think she is not just as evil? Just as broken?"

I nod. "She is certainly broken," I admit. "But she is not evil. Everything she has done, every bad thing, was for a purpose. All of it was for me. Killing you? She did it to save me. To save herself."

"Lies! You always were a pathetic fool. So naïve." He's hysterical now. I have his life in my hands, and he's powerless. If there is one thing Reahgan cannot stand its powerlessness. "It's no wonder father hated you," he screeches. "Even if you were his blood, he'd hate you. He'd hate you how I do."

I clench my jaw, anger and pain swirling inside, but I do not react.

"Fine, I was going to play the nice big brother, but if

you both must die—so be it!" He snarls and then pushes against me. He's calling my bluff because all I have to do is not move and his soul would be destroyed, my iron blade severing his connection to this earth.

But I pull my blade back and allow him to leap away.

He spins past me, toward the swamp—toward Caelynn. I throw my iron blade at his flying form, right over her fallen body. He hisses again, dodges the blade, and flits away.

My hands are trembling, my magic running low, and the wraiths surrounding us have begun their descent toward us.

Caelynn gasps as I quickly grab her, one arm gently beneath her head and the other beneath her knees. She winces and whines as I pick her broken body up and carry her to the cottage.

# 57
## CAELYNN

Rev lays me on the bed gently. "Rev," I say stupidly. What else do I say when he just protected me, his enemy, against his beloved brother? "I'm sorry."

He shrugs. "I made a choice."

I bite my lip, remembering those same words from the trials. Only this time, he chose *me*. I swallow, unsure what that even means.

"Thank you," I whisper and close my eyes. I don't know how long it will take to heal from an injury like this. Even with a partial healing it could take a week or more. Reahgan had my heart in his grip—literally. He could have killed me. Would have, if he hadn't wanted to drag it out. He wanted me to suffer. And Rev too.

I can still feel him. His magic clenches over my chest. It's not enough to kill me but enough to keep me miserable for an extended period of time.

Rev gets to work boarding up the shattered window, and he carves a new symbol into the wood.

"That's not going to keep him out, is it?"

Rev shrugs. "Luminescent magic seems to work very well against wraiths. The ward may not hold against my brother, but it'll help. And I'll protect you if he does come back."

I swallow and allow myself a moment to revel in those words. But they only go so deep because the truth is not much has changed.

He chose me. Which is wonderful for my heart. But… Reahgan was still right. I need to die for this to all be over. I have what they need, and until I'm dead and gone, the war will continue.

And we are both still trapped in the Schorchedlands with no way out. Only one of us can escape this wicked prison.

"Rev," I say, eyeing the iron blade sitting on the ground beside the bed… How could I say those words, the words on the tip of my tongue, to the male who just chose me over his brother? How could I kill myself now?

Seeming to read my thoughts, Rev saunters across the small cottage and looks me in the eye. "You're not dying, Cae."

The corner of my lip ticks up at the use of that name, but it falls quickly. "He was right," I say, plunging us both in icy despair. I can feel it in the air, settling between us. I know he feels it too. "If I were to die…"

"No," he says firmly. "I know the only way you've found to solve things in your life has been to give away pieces of yourself. But that's not how this is going to work. You're done. You hear me?" His eyes flash to the blade. He grips it quickly. "They want us apart. But we're stronger together. We'll find a way to kill those bastards. You and me."

I can't help but smile.

"Besides," he leans forward placing his knee between my legs and leans in, pressing the iron blade to my neck gently, "if anyone is going to kill you, it's me." The edge of the dull blade slides all the way down my neck to my collarbone. I shiver and close my eyes.

Then, he drops the blade, and his lips crash onto mine. My lips part in surprise, eyes fly open. I grip the back of his head, holding him tightly to me. His delicious taste on my tongue.

He pulls away too quickly, leaving me breathless and more confused than ever.

His fingers find the hem of my shirt, and he drags it up slowly exposing my stomach and finally pulling the fabric away from the raging hole in my chest. I wince and whine as the bloody cloth is pulled away.

His grey eyes hold my gaze as his hand slides from my hip up my stomach until his palm hovers over the wound. My chest heaves desperately.

Then, magic burns as it tears me apart and stitches me back together. I moan in a mixture of pain and pleasure, throwing my head back and arching my back at the flood of fiery pleasure

"Have I mentioned I really like it when you do that?" His husky voice sends another wave of pleasure and desire through my body.

His powerful heat subsides after another moment, and I'm left gasping for breath. He rolls onto his back beside me.

"That's all I get?" I lick my lips.

He chuckles and then sits up. "We both need to rest."

I swallow, pushing down all my desire and questions at once. He leans in and slips his arm under my head then presses soft lips to my forehead. I sigh and curl into his side.

As much as I'm loath to admit he's right, I can already feel my body slipping into a warm haze of sleep.

"We'll figure this out, Cae. I'm not leaving you here."

It's a stupid hope—that we could somehow both be free of this cursed place—but with Rev's arms around me and his magic still singing inside my chest, surrounding my healing heart, I allow myself to believe it. If only for the night.

———

Continue Caelynn and Rev's story in Soul of Thorns.

Keep reading for a sneak peak at the free prequel novella about Caelynn's bargain with the Nightbringer.

# A TERRIBLE BARGAIN
## AN IMPOSSIBLE CHOICE

**Kill my soul mate or lose my life**

Caelynn adores her homelands in the Shadow Court,

but as the one of the poorest and weakest courts in the realm there's little opportunity for a talented fae like her.

When she overhears her parents planning to force her into another court, she runs away—straight to the Cave of Mysteries to jump start her initiation. She'll become a shadow fae with or without permission.

But there are monsters in those deep tunnels. The Night Bringer is waiting for her, and once she's in his clutches she must complete his bargain or accept eternal slavery.

But this bargain is no simple task. The Night Bringer dresses her like a princess and sends her to a ball to kill a fae prince. A prince who just so happens to be her soul mate.

Keep reading for a sneak peak

———

# NIGHT BRINGER
## CHAPTER 1

I hold my hand out in front of me, and an inky black smoke swirls over my palm. It pops and sizzles, twisting and then finally—squawks. Well, it's actually more like a squeal.

The boy behind me chuckles. I ignore him, watching my creation with wonder.

The smoke creature's wings are sharp bone covered in smooth leathery skin. His nose pushed up into an ugly grimace.

"Caelynn," Madam Romor chides. "You were meant to make a raven—not a bat!"

More laughter choruses from behind me. I smile and flick an eyebrow.

The black smoke continues to shift and dissolve beneath my charmed bat. It rises into the sky with rapid flapping until it darts behind the black leaves of the shadow maple and back. He swipes down toward a black-haired girl who screams and ducks down. He swings around and lands in my open palm.

I shrug. "I like him."

"It's not about liking, Caelynn. It's about following directions and completing magic with intention. If you let your magic rule you, you'll find it can take over your mind and soul."

I roll my eyes. *So dramatic.*

"That's a fail, Caelynn."

"What?" My mouth falls open. "It was perfect! My magic was fantastic!"

"Your magic was average, and the fact that you didn't follow directions means I have no idea if you intended to make a bat. I have to assume you simply failed at creating a raven."

"You know that's not what happened."

"I most definitely do not."

I clench my fists. "Then let me try again," I say through my teeth.

She nods, her expression somber. "Tomorrow you can prove yourself. Today you get a zero."

I throw my hands up. "That's not fair. I can't afford a zero!" Well, I could, if it were up to me. But my parents? They're going to be so angry.

"We can talk about this later. Gordon, it's your turn."

"But—"

"SIT, Caelynn. Your time is through."

Gordon stands, his hands in his pocket and eyes cast to the ground.

I wrinkle my nose, debating between sending an army of ravens to attack Madam Romor and hiding my emotions. I hate letting people see my fear. I swallow down my panic, and I sit on the black blades of grass, letting them tickle my palm as a calming distraction.

Behind us, the Whisperwood looms. The Crumbling Mountain is only barely visible beyond them. Our magic is strong here where natural elemental power surges from the trees. There is a dirt pathway lined by shiny onyx wires leading the way. One direction takes you deep into the whispering forest, and the other takes you back to my village.

It's a quaint town. The most remarkable element is its proximity to the Whisperwood—my favorite place in the world. Well, besides maybe the Shadow Court Palace, but I wouldn't know. I've never been. It's a distant dream to go there, and I am so close I can taste it. To be invited to the palace by the queen herself...

I sigh.

I'm old enough to qualify for an invite. I'm strong enough. Smart enough.

But not trusted, not by my parents.

Because first I must pass the two rites of passage of my court, and as of now, my parents haven't allowed it. And a zero today in communal magic lessons isn't going to do me much good in changing their mind.

Since it's such a small town, our classes are small too.

There are only eleven fae still attending classes. Seven boys, four girls. We meet in the meadow outside the Whisperwood twice a week for lessons. The rest of the time, I'm schooled by my family. Which...doesn't always go so well. My mom hates trying to "wrangle" me, as she calls it.

I cross my arms and watch as Gordon makes a perfect raven. It hardly moves at all, just rustles its shimmering black feathers and blinks a few times. It doesn't even squawk.

"Wonderful!" Madam Romor says.

I roll my eyes.

"Kayne. Your turn."

Kayne looks my way, his dark eyes shadowed with mischief. He winks before approaching our teacher. He's only two months older than me and has already completed his first rite of passage—passing the Black Gates. He has one more before he'll be invited to the palace to meet the queen. Then he'll be considered a full Shadow Court fae.

He should ace this lesson no problem.

When he stands and holds out a hand, black magic crackles like a storm, and a little blueish-black bat drops onto his palm. I suck in an amazed breath.

"Kayne," Madam Romor says, her voice low. "What is this?"

His bat darts through the students sitting on the grass, and I laugh as it tickles my ear. Kayne winks in my direction.

"I liked him too. Wanted one of my own," he tells Madam Romor.

Her mouth falls wide, eyes darting to me and then back. He's one of her favorites, despite the fact that he's more of a trouble maker than I am. Truth be told, it's a prized attribute among fae. Madam Romor is just less forgiving when it comes to me.

Kayne has learned to cover his misdeeds better than I have, and his magic is stronger than average in our kingdom.

If Madam gives me a zero, she'll have to give Kayne one too. And she hates it. I can see it in her eyes.

There are fifteen total courts in our world. The Shadow Court is considered one of the "lessers"—meaning we aren't strong. We have no influence in rulemaking. We aren't invited to important events. We don't even have a member on the queen's council, but the eight ruling courts get one each.

So, any powerful fae in these lands are prized. Strong women are vulnerable. Their talents are often hidden or diminished, because for generations, the High King would marry them off to other courts, often against their will. For a time, the shadow fae stupidly obliged, thinking it would earn us back the High Court's good graces. It started long before we were officially stripped of the title of "ruling" court which only happened a century ago, but we've been "unofficially" condemned by the High Courts for much longer.

It's been almost eight hundred years since we last had a High Court ruler and three hundred since we had a member on the council.

The Shadow Court rulers have been desperate to earn back our place as one of the ruling courts, and so they gave the other courts whatever they wanted. Even their own citizens, thinking it would help.

It didn't, and eventually, selling off our strongest females had a massive impact on our nation's power. First, they called us weak and then they manipulated us into giving away what power we did hold. The most magically gifted children were born to anyone but us.

The realm is afraid of us. Our dark power, our ability to

wield secrets like a blade, so they kept us weak. But dark doesn't mean evil. It's a color. Shadow is simply our element. Nothing more. I'm no more evil than the fairy godmother my Nan tells me about in her human nursery rhymes.

Madam Romor loves Kayne for his power. She hates me for my cheek—or maybe it's because my father's brother married off his daughter to the Glistening Court, and she thinks the same will be done to me.

I suppose I might be bitter too, if I had to teach an adolescent I thought would inevitably go to another court, making my teachings pointless.

But I won't let anyone send me away. I am a shadow fae. I belong in the Shadow Court. I won't let them sell me off like cattle—not that my father would ever do that to me.

If there is one thing in the world I want, it's to show them all.

I'm not weak.

Our court isn't weak.

And maybe, just maybe, they're right to fear us.

# NIGHT BRINGER
## CHAPTER 2

I slip into my cottage, head ducked low. Our home is small—only two rooms total: my parent' room and *everything else.* Funny because my father is technically a count.

This dank little cottage is a pretty sad abode from someone of his ranking. He owns a massive manor a few miles north of here. It just happens to be entirely uninhabitable, left to crumble in disrepair because we don't have the ability to fuel it.

Magic is our world's currency, well kind of. It's what makes our world run. Trade is done with magic-filled gemstones, but our magic thrums through everything, like blood through the veins of the body of our kingdom. Everything is run by magic, running water, light, farming, and even most of our structures are held together by it.

Without magic, it all falls apart, and we… don't have much.

Which is why my father moved to the village where the

natural magic of the Whisperwood could fuel our basic needs and make our lives easier.

I don't mind living more humbly than my birth suggests, but this small cottage does mean I get very little privacy. But I do have a nook in the corner with a couple shelves and a blanket on the ground. That's my one spot I can—sometimes—"get away". That's where I head now, tiptoeing across the uneven stone floor.

"How was class?" I jump at my father's voice as he calls from my parents' bedroom.

"Fine," I squeak and curl up behind my bookshelf.

"You sure about that?" he asks, his voice low but closer. I grab a book—any book—and hide my nose behind it.

"Of course."

He marches across the room slowly. "Because you only ever run straight to your books if something bad happened." He leans against my shelf, staring down at me.

I bite my lip. He's going to find out anyway. Madam Romor reports to all the parents each week. If I lie to him now, he'll be even angrier when he does find out.

"Madam Romor gave me a zero," I blurt out.

"A zero?" His eyebrows rise.

"Yes, but it was completely ridiculous. I made a perfect bat that squawked and swooped around at will."

"So, why a zero then?"

"Because she told us to make a raven." I shrug. "I didn't see what was so wrong about..."

"Part of class is learning to take direction. We've talked about that, Cae."

"Yeah, I know."

He shakes his head and walks back toward the water basin.

Truth is, classes are entirely meaningless. There is no reason my folks should even care about high marks or low marks. It's your rites of passage and overall reputation that affect future success. But for some reason, it really matters to them. They always act so disappointed in me when I don't do well.

Relieved by the surprisingly short conversation with my father, I drop the book I used to hide and pick another to actually read and drift away from reality for a while.

Unfortunately, I lack the focus needed to get too into it. History books aren't particularly kind to my homeland, so most shadow folk ignore them or only read those few written from our perspective. I am one of the few that is fascinated by the rest of the fae world. Actually, I'm fascinated by all worlds—even the tales my gran tells me about the human world. She's fully fae, as are the rest of my family, but she spent several years in the human world. There's a portal to that magicless place near the seashore and adult fae are allowed to travel there if they desire— most don't, or if they do it's only for a couple years out of pure curiosity. Occasionally, banishment to that world is a punishment handed down by the High Courts for dangerous criminals.

My Nan was there for almost a decade and she was actually a famous singer in a land called Hollywood, until she faked her death and came back home. She tells me about some of the fae that still live there, never aging, always beautiful, and the humans are none-the-wiser.

That's always been hard for me to believe. They age so quickly! How could a fae stay there for forty years as the same person without humans noticing anything strange? She says celebrities get away with it, somehow.

Anyway, I keep a few history books from my own world because that's even more fascinating to me. I have books from the Luminescent Court, Flicker Court and Glistening Court, which is where my cousin now lives. I don't usually think much of her since I never even met her, but being married off to another kingdom sounds...traumatizing. A betrayal of the worst kind. Did she want it? Did she fight it?

Those three courts are considered "ruling" courts. And their perception of my homeland is less than kind.

One day, I want to change that. One day, I want them all to see how powerful and wonderful shadow fae can be.

One day, I want to prove them all wrong.

I duck my head lower behind my shelf as the door to the cottage opens and closes. My mother begins talking with my father about her trip to the market. She bought some wheat to make shade bread and seeds and pears for our dinner salad.

I fully expect my father to tell my mother about my zero, but suddenly he breaks into news about the Luminescent Court, and my ears perk up. He tells her about a ball this weekend to celebrate the choosing of the new High Heir.

In the fae world, the High Ruler changes every one hundred years, a different court each time. The current High Queen is from the Flicker Court. The news broke last week that she'd chosen her successor to be the prince from the Luminescent Court.

For us, in the forgotten land of shadows, it's unexciting news. We haven't had the opportunity to have a ruler for several hundred years. They picked another ruling court heir. *Big whoop.* But a ball does sound rather exciting...

"Invitations went out yesterday."

My mother chuckles. "And we didn't get one," she says in exaggerated horror. "How scandalous!"

"No one in the shadow realm got one."

There's a pause. "Not even our Queen?" My mother's tone is low, serious.

"Not even the Queen of the Whisperwood," my father agrees. For several moments, there is only shuffling as my mother prepares her supplies for our meal. That is indeed big news.

Our Queen is beloved in the Shadow Court, but it's well known that she isn't magically gifted. Since power can trickle down from the high rankings to the people, this puts us at a strong disadvantage. But...there isn't anyone better. So even if she were to abandon the royal bloodline for a new heir, it wouldn't help.

If even out queen was left out of a major event... it means our court is falling even further out of favor with the rest of the realm—which is saying something.

"Is Cae home yet?" My mother asks after a while.

The conversation turns to hushed tones, and I bite my lip. Ahh, yes, here comes the inevitable. My father whispers his tale to my mother, and my stomach sinks.

"You're joking," my mother says. "Caelynn!"

I suck in a breath.

"Get out here now!"

I bite my lip and stand, slinking slowly toward my parents standing by the hearth.

"What do you have to say for yourself?"

What could I say? That I'm actually one of the best in my class, so they should stop worrying about me? That grades don't matter?

I sigh. "I'll do better next time." And do the most boring, easy, unoriginal magic I can possibly manage because that's what impresses my teacher the most.

"Yes, you will. And... you'll be staying home during the Yareakh festival next weekend."

"What?" I shout. "Are you kidding me?" Yareakh is one of the few Shadow Court festivals. It commemorates the building of the palace and the beginning of our kingdom many thousands of years ago. This little town transforms into something else entirely for days. We all wear costumes and decorate our homes with moon flowers and glowing Lumi seeds. We have a huge silver fire in the middle of the town square and play music and drink tonic and dance.

The town match maker—someone trained to recognize mate bonds—will run around placing oil of varying colors on unmarried fae's hands. If you find a match in color, you're meant to kiss beneath the moonlight. It's silly but fun. I kissed Kayne last year, and he's been nicer to me ever since. I wonder if that's why he winked at me today. Does he think we'll be matched again this year?

Rumor has it, if you're matched with the same fae twice in a row, you're fated mates.

Also silly. With only a few dozen unmarried fae in the village, the chances of being matched twice aren't that low but the chances of your mate being from the same small village is.

"Mama," I say low and fierce. Keeping me from the festival would be cruel and damaging to my reputation. "You can't do that, and you know it."

She purses her lips, eyes set. She does know it, she's planning to stick with it all the same. *Stubborn fool.*

"Marks in school are meaningless. That celebration is everything!"

There is a reason we choose that night to dance beneath the moonlight. Because it's the most magic-filled night of the year for Shadow Fae. It builds our magic, helps to fuel the town for another year and can even build magic within young fae like me.

Taking that away from me is worse than me making low marks in class.

Even my father looks concerned. He doesn't like to disagree with my mother in front of me—he waits until the sun sets and we head to bed. Even though I can hear every word through our rickety walls.

"Corolla—"

Her harsh eyes carve into him. "She can reverse this decision by doing well in her courses. Both at home and communal."

My father presses his lips into a thin line. He doesn't like this any more than I do. Good, at least he's thinking rationally.

"That's final. Now go wash up before our meal."

"I'm not hungry," I say, then march to my corner and hide the rest of the day away.

———

Tears sting my eyes as I listen to my parents' whispered conversation during dinner time. Do they really think I can't hear them?

First, my mother insists I need consequences and nothing else they could take away would bother me enough for sufficient motivation. My father says keeping me away from the festival could ruin my entire future.

"If she's to remain in this court, she needs the magic of the festival, and she needs this community."

"She doesn't need that magic as much as she needs to blend in. Standing out is a danger. Isn't that what you said?"

I purse my lips. *What does that mean?*

"What do you think is going to happen to her by disobeying a simple lesson?"

"If we allow her to disobey her lessons what else could she disobey? A willful child in her position is..."

Does my mother's voice sound...scared?

"She doesn't need the kind of discipline you're so determined she learns to belong here."

"But if she had the power needed—"

"And you think she has it?" My father spits, cutting her off. "You think she has enough magic to gain attention? Even with the Yareakh's favor, she's too weak."

I can't stop the gasp that leaves my throat. My father thinks I'm weak?

*My father thinks I'm weak.* I shake my head, tears stinging my eyes.

"Neither you nor I are impressive in our magical abilities," my mother says in a lower tone. "We always assumed she would be the same but..."

"You're being paranoid, Corolla. She isn't that strong that we need to worry. We need to allow her to follow through with the cultural rites or... or come up with a new plan. Perhaps with a pairing, she could have a chance—"

"With what pairing? The Windshade boy? What happens if she's matched with him again?"

My father sighs. "He would be a good match."

"Yes, it's a good match and usually I'd be thrilled for that potential but he's the strongest boy in town. And she may blend in fine if we allow her to follow the path she's on. But what about her children?"

My father sighs. "So then what? We suppress her? For how long? To what end? I thought we'd decided not to find her a match elsewhere. Have you changed your mind?"

I gasp. *A match elsewhere?* He couldn't possibly mean to another court, could he?

"We did agree." My mother's voice goes lower, a whisper as soft as the wind. "But... well, I don't know. Perhaps we should consider it."

I peek over the shelf to see my father nod slowly.

*No.*

"I still have connections," he says so lowly I'm not sure if I'm hearing him correctly. He can't possibly be saying what I think he is. "If we keep her from the next rite, we will have time to see if something can be done."

My jaw drops and tears well in my eyes. I won't let them do that. I can't.

I love the shadowlands, and I won't let anyone take them away from me.


Read the full story for free: https://dl.bookfunnel.com/t5ec9u1rot

# A NOTE FROM THE AUTHOR

Thank you so much for spending your time reading my books and getting to know these characters. It means so much! This series was both wonderful and stressful to write (we were smack in the middle of a pandemic at the time!) but it's been so fulfilling.

I'd love it if you left a review. They help authors more than you realize

If you'd like to learn more about my books and get updates on my new releases please join my newsletter.

Join my newsletter here!
Join my reader group!

And lastly—I'd love to hear from you. Be my friend!
Instagram
Twitter
Facebook

# ACKNOWLEDGMENTS

First, thank you to my husband, Sean. Indie publishing is so much more of a commitment than what we've been used to (because I had to do nearly EVERYTHING myself). Thank you for supporting this dream of mine.

Thank you to Lisa Murray Kroger and Madeline Dyer for your awesome feedback! Karen Meeus and Claudia Frazer for assisting in proofreading!

Thank you to Kelley York for the lovely cover and Cait Marie at Functionally Fiction for copy editing!

All my newsletter and everyone at Stacey's Page Turners members for helping me to name characters and overall being supporting and amazing people! I couldn't do this without you!!!

All the awesome indie author Facebook groups, especially Queens of the Quill! Can't wait to read all of your fae books!!!

# ABOUT THE AUTHOR

Stacey Trombley is a casino pit boss by night, YA author by day. She lives in Ohio with her husband, son, and GSD Riley. When she's not writing or reading her husband is probably dragging her along on one of his crazy adventures for this travel vlog or competing against him about who can pick the most Survivor winners in the first episode (hint: she's winning). But mostly, she's probably reading.

www.ingramcontent.com/pod-product-compliance
Lightning Source LLC
Chambersburg PA
CBHW051306130726
47987CB00004B/1693